**Disney**

# HIGH SCHOOL MUSICAL

## THE ENCORE EDITION

# Disney

# HIGH SCHOOL MUSICAL

## THE ENCORE EDITION

**DISNEY PRESS**

Los Angeles • New York

PRESENTING

Disney

# HIGH SCHOOL MUSICAL

The Junior Novel
Adapted by N. B. Grace

Based on the Disney Channel Original Movie
*High School Musical*, written by Peter Barsocchini

EAST HIGH

ROCK

STAR

SMILE

# CHAPTER 1

It was a magical New Year's Eve at a vacation resort in the mountains. Gleaming white snow covered the ground, stars sparkled in the crisp, clear air, and everyone was beginning to get in the party mood.

Everyone, that is, except Troy Bolton and his father, Jack, who were still on the basketball court, playing one-on-one. They were covered with sweat, but they were having too much fun to stop.

Troy had the ball, and he was doing a good job of getting around his dad. After all, Troy was on the high school basketball team. Not only that, he was the team captain. He had the smooth moves and explosive action of a real star.

But Jack was more than just Troy's dad. Jack was also the basketball team's coach. So Mr. Bolton gave his son advice as they played.

"Keep working left, Troy," Mr. Bolton said. "The guy guarding you in the championship game won't expect that. You'll torch him."

Troy nodded, breathing hard. "By going left—" he said.

"He'll look middle, you take it downtown," his dad—and coach—explained.

Troy nodded again. "Like this?"

He spun past his father, jumped, and sunk a reverse layup. The ball whistled cleanly through the basket. Nothing but net!

His father grinned. "Sweet."

Troy grinned back. Nothing felt better than playing basketball when you were in the groove!

They could have played all night, but just then Troy's mom walked into the gym. She was wearing a sequined party dress and clearly had things other than B-ball on her mind.

"Boys? Hello?" she called. Once she got their attention, she went on. "Did we really fly all this way to play more basketball?"

Troy and his father glanced at each other slyly. They knew she didn't really want an answer to that question, but they gave her one anyway. In perfect unison, they shrugged and said, "Yeah."

Mrs. Bolton gave an exasperated sigh. "It's the last night of vacation. The party . . . ? Remember?"

Actually, they had both totally forgotten the big New Year's Eve party that the resort was holding, but they knew it wasn't wise to admit that.

"Oh, right, right," Mr. Bolton said quickly. "New Year's Eve." He hesitated, then asked, with some fear, "Do we have to wear funny hats?"

"Absolutely," she said firmly. "And we're due in half an hour. Troy, they have a kids' party downstairs in the Freestyle Club."

"Kids' party?" Troy protested. That made him sound like a toddler!

"Young adults," his mom quickly amended. "Now go shower up.

With heavy sighs, Troy and his father did as she said.

As Troy took one last glance at the basketball court, he thought, The championship game is in a couple of weeks! I should be practicing, not going to some stupid "kids' party"! Besides, how much fun could hanging out with a bunch of kids possibly be. . . .

Meanwhile, in another part of the lodge, another mother was about to tear her daughter away from a different fascinating activity.

Gabriella Montez was comfortably curled up in an overstuffed chair in the sitting area. She was enjoying the peace and quiet—everyone else was already at the party—and had totally lost herself in a book called *If You Only Knew Me*. It was the best book she had read since, well, since the last book she checked out of the library, and she couldn't wait to get to the end.

However, she didn't even get to the next page. The book was lifted right out of her hands, and she looked up to see her mother standing over her.

"Gabby, it's New Year's Eve," Mrs. Montez said. "Enough reading."

"But, Mom, I'm almost done and—" Gabriella protested.

Her mother just shook her head. "There's a teen party," she said firmly. "I've laid out your best dress. Go."

Gabriella eyed her mother's sparkly party dress and sighed. She knew when she was defeated.

She nodded, but asked, "Can I have my book back?"

Her mother handed it over and Gabriella headed toward her room to change. As soon as she was out of her mom's sight, however, she opened the book and began reading as she walked.

She might have to go to some stupid teen party, she thought, but she didn't plan to turn her brain off until the very last minute.

**A** short time later, Troy and Gabriella were in the teen club, feeling out of place. It was packed with kids wearing goofy party hats, blowing on noisemakers, and laughing.

Everyone else seems to be having fun, Troy thought glumly. He had showered and dressed in nice pants and a pressed shirt, but he just wished he was back on the basketball court.

In another part of the room, Gabriella sat by herself, wearing black jeans and a cute sweater. I could be back in my room, reading, Gabriella thought wistfully. I was just getting to the good part, too.

Neither one of them was having any fun at all.

Most of the kids in the room were watching a karaoke contest that was in full swing on a raised stage. As two teenagers finished their song, the emcee called out cheerfully, "How about that for a couple of snowboarders?!"

The audience applauded, and the emcee started looking around the room, trying to spot anyone else who was willing to sing karaoke to a room full of strangers. Spotlights swirled over the crowd, and the music played even louder to get the partygoers' adrenaline pumping.

"All right," the emcee said into his mike. "Let's see who is gonna rock the house next. . . ."

That was the cue. The music stopped. The two spotlights picked out the next karaoke "volunteers."

One spotlight was on Troy.

The other was on Gabriella.

Both looked startled, and even a little terrified. They shook their heads, but it was no use. The emcee jumped into the crowd and pulled them up onto the stage.

Troy and Gabriella were mortified. Somehow— they weren't quite sure how it happened— microphones were put in their hands. There they were, stuck. Onstage. The center of attention. And no way to escape.

Before either one of them could actually faint or throw up from fear, the music started.

Well, here goes, Troy thought with resignation. Might as well make the best of it . . .

He started singing, softly and carefully. He could barely get the words out. It was all he could do to read the lyrics on the screen of the karaoke machine and try to stay in tune. He sang:

*"Livin' in my own world*
*Didn't understand*
*That anything can happen*
*When you take a chance"*

No one seemed to be paying much attention to them. That was a *good* thing, Gabriella thought. And, after all, if this boy was willing to risk public humiliation, she might as well be a good sport and try to sing, too.

She opened her mouth and began singing. Although her voice was just above a whisper, it was sweet and pure. She sang:

*"I never believed in*
*What I couldn't see*
*I never opened my heart*
*To all the possibilities"*

All right, she thought. I can do this. It's not too terrible.

Okay, Troy thought. At least people aren't throwing things at us.

Still, they were too nervous to really belt out the song. They kept singing though, alternating the lines of the ballad.

Finally, they looked at each other, hoping for a little help from their partner in embarrassment.

As they really saw each other, they both experienced something they never had before.

Troy felt a spark of electricity run over his skin. Gabriella felt a warm glow flood through her body. They smiled and, for the first time, began singing to each other. They sang more loudly, more boldly, with more self-assurance.

Suddenly, everyone in the room started to notice: there was something special going on up onstage! Kids began crowding around the edge of the stage, listening and swaying to the music. And now Troy and Gabriella were starting to enjoy themselves. Their nervousness was forgotten as they smiled into each other's eyes.

Before long, they were dancing across the stage and back again, as confident as if they were performing at an arena. As they moved to the music, they never took their eyes off each other.

When the song was over, the crowd applauded and cheered. Troy and Gabriella smiled, breathless and a little stunned by what had just happened.

Troy leaned over and said, "I'm Troy."

Gabriella nodded. "Gabriella."

Neither one of them could stop smiling. Both of them felt an excited, fizzy feeling inside, as if the world had just become a lot more fun.

# CHAPTER 2

They were still giddy from the excitement of their impromptu performance, so they went for a walk outside in the cold, sparkling air.

"You have an awesome voice," Troy said. "You're a singer, right?"

Gabriella shrugged. "Just the church choir is all." She smiled and admitted, "I tried to do a solo and nearly fainted."

"Why's that?" he asked, surprised.

She shook her head at the memory. "I took one look at all the people staring only at me, and the next thing I knew, I was staring at the ceiling. End of solo career."

"The way you sang just now, that's hard to believe," he said sincerely.

"This is the first time I've done something like this," she answered.

Troy knew how she felt. "Completely," he agreed.

"You sound like you've done a lot of singing, too," she said.

"Oh, sure, lots," he said jokingly. "My shower-head is very impressed with me."

At that moment, everyone around them started chanting in unison: "Ten! Nine! Eight! . . ."

The New Year's Eve countdown had begun.

Troy and Gabriella glanced at each other, then just as quickly looked away.

"Seven! Six! Five! Four! . . ."

This was a magical night, Gabriella thought, wishing it would last longer.

I can't believe I didn't want to come to this party, Troy thought. This was awesome!

"Three! Two! One!"

Everyone began cheering and blowing on their noisemakers. Fireworks burst in the sky in showers of red, gold, and blue. Everyone was celebrating—but Troy and Gabriella were suddenly feeling awkward.

People kiss each other on New Year's Eve, Troy thought. Should I—?

It's a tradition to kiss when the clock strikes midnight, Gabriella thought. Will he—?

Neither one moved. After a few seconds, she smiled and said, "I guess I'd better go find my mom and wish her Happy New Year."

Troy nodded. The spell was broken, and he was a little relieved. "Me, too," he said. "I mean, not *your* mom—my mom . . . and dad. I'll call you tomorrow."

He pulled out his cell phone, quickly snapped a picture of her, then handed her the phone.

"Put your number in."

Gabriella grabbed her own phone and handed it to him. "You, too—"

They quickly switched phones and tapped in their numbers. Then Gabriella turned to leave. Troy stopped her.

"Singing with you was the most fun I've had this vacation," he said sincerely. "Where do you—"

Another series of fireworks exploded overhead, drowning out whatever he was saying.

Gabriella was already at the stairs. She waved back, smiling, then vanished. Troy stood absolutely still, gazing after her.

A week later, school had started again at East High School in Albuquerque, New Mexico. It was the first morning back after winter vacation, and the scene was bedlam. Kids were piling out of buses, yelling at each other, showing off new clothes.

As Troy entered the courtyard, under the banner that read "Happy New Year, Wildcats," other students gave him high fives, low fives, and side fives.

His friend and basketball teammate Chad came up to him, yelling, "Yo, doggie! Troy, my hoops boy!"

Chad had wild, curly hair and a wired attitude to match. He was the loyal number two to Troy's number one and, before Troy could blink, he found that Chad had drawn in all the other members of the team. They were happy to see him,

excited to be back together, and totally keyed u[p]
about the championship game, now just a couple
of weeks away.

"Hey, Chad," Troy said. He waved at the other
players. "Dudes . . . Happy New Year."

"Oh, yes, it will be a Happy Wildcat New Year,"
Chad shouted. "Because in two weeks we are
going to the championships, with you leading us
to infinity and beyond!"

Troy laughed, and the other members of the
Wildcat basketball team nodded and high-fived
each other. Chad was right. They were about to
fulfill their destiny!

At that moment, Sharpay and Ryan Evans
pushed their way through the basketball posse.
Both of them tossed their hair as only copresidents of the Drama Club could.

As usual, Sharpay looked Barbie-doll perfect,
with blown-out hair, full makeup, and fashionable
clothes. Her brother, Ryan, looked just as hip.

Zeke, one of the basketball players, watched
Sharpay as she haughtily pushed her way through
the crowd. "Hey, the ice princess has returned
from the North Pole," he muttered to his crew.

"Yeah, she probably spent the holidays the way she always does," Chad said.

Jason, another basketball player, willingly filled the role of straight man. "How's that?" he asked.

"Shopping for mirrors!" Chad cracked.

He howled like a wolf in appreciation of his own joke. His teammates joined in.

Still howling, they walked by Taylor McKessie, the president of the Chemistry Club, who was accompanied by a few of her brainiac friends.

Taylor scornfully eyeballed the basketball players, then said to her friends, "Ah, behold the zoo animals heralding the new year. How tribal."

As her friends haughtily agreed, the bell rang and everybody hurried to their homerooms.

The crowds had thinned somewhat as Principal Matsui walked down the hall, escorting a new student. It was a nervous Gabriella and her mother, who were trying to listen as the principal gave them his sales pitch.

"We're consistently rated in the top ten academically in the state, and I think you'll also find this a wonderful community atmosphere," Principal Matsui said.

Gabriella tried to smile as she peeked in a window in a classroom door. The scene inside was total, first-day-back-at-school chaos. Her stomach flipped over and she cast an appealing look at her mother.

"Mom, my stomach—"

"—is always nervous on the first day at a new school," her mother finished reassuringly. "You'll do great, you always do. And I've made my company promise that I can't be transferred again until you graduate."

Gabriella smiled weakly. This was always the worst part, she reminded herself.

"Worry not, Gabriella," Principal Matsui said. "I've reviewed your impressive transcripts. I expect your light will shine very brightly here at East High."

Gabriella knew he was trying to be helpful, but her stomach twisted even more at these words. "I don't want to be the school freaky genius girl again," she whispered to her mom.

Mrs. Montez hugged her. "Just be Gabriella," she said warmly.

Gabriella went to her homeroom with Ms.

Darbus, the school's drama teacher. True to her theatrical background, she was flamboyantly dressed in a long, flowing dress and wore oversized glasses.

Gabriella quickly took her seat, doing her best to be invisible. She didn't see Troy enter with his best bud, Chad—but as Troy said hello to other students, he caught a glimpse of her from the corner of his eye.

Surprised, he craned his neck for a better look, but other students kept getting in the way. That girl, he thought. She looked just like—but what would the girl from New Year's Eve be doing here . . . ?

Before he could get a better look, the final bell rang and everybody scrambled to sit at their desks.

Ms. Darbus stood in front of the class as if she were taking center stage in a Broadway theater. "I trust you all had splendid holidays," she said. "Check the sign-up sheets in the lobby for new activities, especially our winter musical. There'll be single auditions for the supporting roles, as well as pairs auditions for our two leads—"

Chad looked around at his basketball team-mates, grinned, and blew a raspberry at the mention of the musical.

Ms. Darbus glared at him. "Mr. Danforth, this is a place of learning, not a hockey arena," she snapped.

Troy was still craning his neck, trying to see the new girl who looked so much like Gabriella. Finally, frustrated, he pulled his cell phone from his pocket and thumbed through the menu.

The photo of Gabriella that he took on New Year's Eve popped up on the screen. He stared at it, remembering that magical night, as Ms. Darbus happily burbled on.

"There is also a final sign-up for next week's Scholastic Decathlon Competition," she said. "Chem Club president Taylor McKessie can answer your questions on that."

Meanwhile, Troy hit the SEND button on his phone. Suddenly, Gabriella's phone started ringing wildly. At first, she didn't even react. After all, who would be calling her?

Sharpay and Ryan grabbed for their phones. After all, wouldn't *every* call be for them?

Ms. Darbus strode to the front of the room, the light of battle in her eyes. "Ah, the cell-phone menace returns to our crucible of learning!" she cried. She grabbed a plastic bucket labeled "Cell-itary Confinement" and held it out to the brother and sister. "Sharpay and Ryan, your phones, please, and I'll see you in detention."

They rolled their eyes, but deposited their phones in the bucket. The ringing, however, went on.

Ms. Darbus's gaze swept the room, searching for the source of the nefarious ring. Blushing, Gabriella fumbled in her backpack. As she finally dug her phone out and started to turn it off, she saw . . . Troy Bolton's photo?

Her eyes widened with surprise and she accidentally hit ANSWER instead of END.

Now Troy was staring in surprise at his phone, where he saw Gabriella's photo. But Ms. Darbus was looming over Gabriella and holding out her plastic bucket.

"We have zero tolerance on cell phones during class," the drama teacher said sternly. "So, we'll get to know each other at detention. Phone, please . . . and welcome to East High, Miss Montez."

As she walked back to the front of the class, she saw Troy holding his phone and held out her bucket. "Mr. Bolton, I see your phone is involved. Splendid, we'll see you in detention, as well."

Troy sighed and dropped his phone in the bucket.

Behind him, Chad protested. "That's not even a possibility, Ms. Darbus, your honor, because we have basketball practice and Troy is—"

Ms. Darbus whirled around and glared at him. "That's fifteen minutes for you, too, Mr. Danforth. Count 'em!"

At the back of the class, Taylor smirked and whispered to one of her brainiac friends, "That could be tough for Chad, since he probably can't count that high."

She should have known better. Ms. Darbus had better hearing than a bat.

"Taylor McKessie," she said sharply. "Fifteen minutes."

Taylor's jaw dropped. She had never had to serve a minute of detention in her entire life!

But it was no use protesting. Ms. Darbus had already whirled around to survey the rest of the class. "Shall the carnage continue? Vacation is over, people. Way over! Any more comments? Questions?"

Jason, one of the basketball players, thought it was about time to restore a good mood to this morning's homeroom. He raised his hand and asked sincerely, "So how were your holidays, Ms. Darbus?"

As everyone looked at him in disbelief, the bell rang. The class bolted for the door, relieved to be free of Darbus rule for the time being.

# CHAPTER 3

Troy waited anxiously in the hall outside Ms. Darbus's homeroom, hanging back as his friends went on to their next classes.

Finally, Gabriella came out, and he walked toward her, hardly able to breathe.

When Gabriella saw him, her eyes widened in disbelief.

She said, "I don't—"

"—believe it," Troy finished in a whisper.

Gabriella nodded. "Me—"

"—either," Troy finished again. "But how . . ."

"My mom's company transferred her here to

Albuquerque," Gabriella explained. She shook her head in disbelief. "I can't believe you live here. I looked for you at the lodge on New Year's Day, but—"

"We had to leave first thing," Troy said, still whispering.

Gabriella looked puzzled. "Why are you whispering?"

He looked a little embarrassed. "Oh, well, my friends know I went snowboarding, but I didn't tell them about the . . . singing . . . thing."

"Too much for them to handle?" she asked knowingly.

"It was . . . cool," Troy said quickly. He didn't want her getting the idea that he hadn't liked their singing debut! "But, my friends—that's not what I do. That was like a . . . different person."

They had reached the lobby, where activity sign-up sheets were posted. Troy pointed at the sheet for the winter musical auditions.

"Now that you've met Ms. Darbus, I'll bet you can't wait to sign up for that," he said grinning.

Gabriella laughed. "I won't be signing up for

*anything* here for a while," she said. "I just want to get to know the school." She glanced at him shyly. "But if you signed up, I'd consider coming to the show."

Troy shook his head. He couldn't even imagine the reaction he'd get if he signed up for the high school musical! "That's completely impossible," he said.

From behind him, Sharpay's voice said sweetly, "What's impossible, Troy? I wouldn't think 'impossible' is even in your vocabulary." As they turned to look at Sharpay, she gestured toward Gabriella. "So nice of you to show our new classmate around."

She raised one eyebrow as she saw Gabriella looking at the musical sign-up sheet. Very deliberately, Sharpay stepped in front of Gabriella and signed her name with a flourish.

In fact, Gabriella noticed, Sharpay's signature took up the entire sign-up sheet!

But Sharpay looked at her, the picture of innocence, and said, "Oh . . . were you going to sign up, too? My brother and I have starred in all of the school's productions, and we really welcome newcomers." She smiled, ever so sweetly, then added, "There are a lot of supporting roles in this show. I'm sure we could find something for you."

"No, no," Gabriella said hastily. "I was just looking over the bulletin board. Lots going on at this school. Wow." I'm babbling, she thought. I have to stop it! Now! She pointed to Sharpay's huge signature. "Nice penmanship," she added weakly, before hurrying away to her next class.

Now that Sharpay had been left alone with Troy, she decided to seize the opportunity. "So, Troy," she said coyly, "I missed you during vacation. What'd you do?"

He shrugged. "Practiced basketball. Snowboarding. More basketball."

Sharpay nodded cheerfully and, using all of her dramatic training to sound as if she really cared, asked, "When's the big game?"

"Two weeks." Troy sounded resolute, determined. Two weeks until we're either champions— or we're not, he thought.

"You're so dedicated," Sharpay said, batting her

eyelashes just a bit. After a moment, she added, "Just like me. I hope you'll come watch me in the musical? Promise?"

Just like Sharpay to bring the conversation back to herself, Troy thought wryly. But he smiled and nodded as he walked away.

A few hours later, Troy and the basketball team had gathered in the gym for practice. Troy and Chad challenged each other by running a pressure drill, while the other boys ran a weave drill.

"Hey, you know that school-musical thing?" Troy asked as he tried to get around Chad. "Is it true you get extra credit just for auditioning?"

"Who cares?" Chad asked as he blocked Troy.

Troy raised one eyebrow and tried to scoot around Chad from the other side. "It's good to get extra credit . . . for college and all," he said, trying to sound casual.

Chad laughed and shook his head. "Do you think LeBron James ever auditioned for his school musical?" he asked mockingly.

"Maybe . . ." Troy said hesitantly.

"Troy, the music in those shows isn't hip-hop or rock or anything essential to the culture," Chad explained patiently. "It's like . . . *show music*. Costumes, makeup." He shuddered. "Frightening."

Troy shrugged, still trying to sound like it was no big deal. "I thought it might be a good laugh. Sharpay is kind of cute, too."

Now Chad looked at him with total disbelief. "So is a mountain lion, but you don't pet them."

Troy nodded, and gave up for the moment. Time to take charge of this practice, he thought. Time to focus. The championship game, he reminded himself sternly, is only weeks away.

He turned to his team. "All right, let's kick it in, run the shuffle drill," he yelled.

The team quickly took their positions and began bouncing basketballs and weaving around one another with the ease developed through hours of practice.

The balls began to bounce and the players began to move across the floor with a rhythmic, percussive movement. And Troy began to call out the practice drills.

*"Coach said to*
*Fake right*
*And break left*
*Watch out for the pick*
*And keep an eye on defense*
*You gotta run the give and go*
*And take the ball to the hole*
*But don't be afraid*
*To shoot the outside 'J'"*

The Wildcats had developed a team motto, and now Troy shouted it out to get his boys pumped up:

*"Just keep ya' head in the game*
*Keep ya' head in the game*
*Just keep ya' head in the game*
*Don't be afraid to shoot the outside 'J'"*

The team members smiled and moved even faster, smoother, better. Troy was a great captain, and he could motivate them like no one else!

Troy grabbed a ball and joined the drills,

dribbling left around one player and right around another, still calling out drills.

When practice ended, everyone took deep breaths, smiling at how great they felt and how great they had looked. The Wildcats were definitely good to go for the championship!

# CHAPTER 4

The next morning, Gabriella sat at a station in the chemistry lab, across the table from Taylor and next to Sharpay. The students were wearing neat white lab coats and busily setting up equipment as the chemistry teacher wrote equations on the blackboard.

Sharpay gave Gabriella a fake smile. Ever so casually, she said, "So, it seemed like you knew Troy Bolton."

Gabriella glanced up briefly, but she was distracted by the teacher, who was solving the equation on the board. "Not really . . . I just asked him for directions," she said, even as she started checking the teacher's work on her scratch pad.

Sharpay raised the wattage of her smile just a bit. "Troy usually doesn't . . . interact . . . with new students."

"Why not?" Gabriella asked, not really listening. She looked at her equation. Hmmm. Her calculation was quite different from the teacher's. Should she say something? Maybe not. People didn't like it when you pointed out their mistakes. . . .

"It's pretty much basketball 24/7 with him," Sharpay said with a little laugh.

Now Gabriella wasn't listening to Sharpay at all. She rechecked her own calculation and murmured, "Pi to the eleventh power."

She thought she had said it quietly, but apparently not quietly enough.

The chemistry teacher turned around. "Yes, Miss Montez?"

"Oh, I'm sorry," Gabriella said, flustered. "I was just—"

Before she could finish her sentence, the

teacher was standing by her chair, looking down at her notebook.

"Pi to the eleventh power?" the teacher said in surprise. "That's quite impossible." Then she whipped out a calculator and started punching in numbers. Across the table, Taylor had her calculator out as well, and was matching the teacher, keystroke for keystroke.

There was a brief, stunned pause. Then the teacher said, "I stand corrected." She turned back to the blackboard to revise her work. Then she looked over her shoulder, smiled warmly at Gabriella, and added, "And welcome aboard."

Gabriella blushed as Taylor stared at her, impressed.

Troy was strolling through the lobby on the way to his next class when he caught sight of the musical audition sign-up sheet. His steps slowed.

It was crazy, he *knew* it was crazy, but he couldn't seem to stop thinking about the musical. He stood still, almost hypnotized by the piece of paper. He was so lost in his thoughts that he didn't notice Sharpay's brother, Ryan, who was hanging out nearby with a couple of the Drama Club kids.

Ryan's eyes narrowed suspiciously. When Troy finally moved on, Ryan ran up to the sheet, just to make sure. . . .

At that moment, Sharpay arrived. Ryan rushed up to her, breathless. "Troy Bolton was looking at our audition list!" he reported.

Sharpay stiffened, all senses suddenly alert. "Again? He was hanging around with that new girl, and they were both looking at the list." She paused a moment to think. "There's something freaky about her," Sharpay decided. "Where did she say she was from?"

Minutes later, Sharpay and Ryan were in the school library, doing an Internet search on Gabriella. A number of articles immediately popped up on the screen.

"Whiz Kid Leads School to Scholastic Championship," read one headline.

"Sun High Marvel Aces Statewide Chemistry Competition," another headline said.

A photo of Gabriella showed her beaming into the camera and holding a number of awards.

As Sharpay printed out the article, Ryan said, "Whoa . . . an Einstein-ette. So why is she interested in our musical?"

"I'm not sure that she is," Sharpay said. "And we needn't concern ourselves with amateurs." She neatly folded the printouts and stood up. "But there's no harm in making certain that Gabriella is welcomed into school activities that are . . . appropriate . . . for her. After all, she loves pi."

And Ryan, who was always at least one step behind Sharpay, saw his sister's smile and knew that she had a plan.

Later that day, everyone who had been given detention had to serve their time.

Ms. Darbus, of course, held her detention on the stage of the school's theater. The detainees' punishment was painting scenery, mopping the stage, and binding scripts.

Sharpay satisfied her requirements by telling Ryan how to paint a prop—and watching as he did it. Chad was trying to assemble a piece of scenery, but he was hopeless. All his agility and finesse on the basketball court translated to total clumsiness when he picked up a hammer. Troy and Gabriella were working on opposite sides of the stage, exchanging shy glances and trying to muster the courage to actually speak to each other.

Before either one of them could seize the moment, however, Taylor entered the auditorium and made a beeline for Gabriella. Taylor looked as if she had just won the lottery—and, considering that she was the Scholastic Club president, maybe she had.

She came to a halt in front of Gabriella and said, beaming, "The answer is yes!"

"Huh?" Gabriella was lost.

"Our Scholastic Decathlon team has its first competition next week, and there's certainly a chair open for you," Taylor said excitedly. She reached into her purse and pulled out a sheaf of newspaper articles about Gabriella's academic achievements.

Gabriella was stunned. "Where did those come from?"

"Didn't you slip them in my locker?" Now Taylor was confused.

"Of course not." Gabriella was more than confused—she was upset. She had wanted to pass for average—well, as close to average as she could. Now that plan was destroyed.

Sharpay stood to one side, pretending not to listen even as she listened as hard as she could.

Taylor quickly regrouped. "Well, we'd love to have you on the team. We meet almost every day after school." Then she had a quick flash of how much better their team would be if Gabriella joined, and added, "Please?"

"I need to catch up on the curriculum here before I think about joining any clubs..." Gabriella started hesitantly.

Sharpay whipped around. If there was any time to join this conversation, she thought, it was now. "But what a perfect way to get caught up, meeting with the smartest kids in the school. What a generous offer, Taylor!"

Gabriella looked from one girl to the other, feeling trapped. She was saved by Ms. Darbus, who walked onto the stage from the wings and said,

"So many new faces in here today." She stared at them meaningfully. "I hope it doesn't become a habit, though the Drama Club can always use an extra hand. Now, as we work, let's probe the mounting evils of cell phones. My first thought on the subject is—"

Chad could recognize the beginning of a boring, long-winded lecture when he heard one. He quickly tried to hide inside a fake tree.

No luck. He could still hear Ms. Darbus, droning on. . . .

As Ms. Darbus listed all the problems with cell phones, the basketball team was taking the court for after-school practice. Coach Bolton entered and blew his whistle for practice to start.

"Okay, let's get rolling. Two weeks to the big—"

Then he paused and looked around. Something was wrong, he thought. Something was missing. Someone was missing. . . .

"Where are Troy and Chad?"

"Perhaps the most heinous example of cell-phone abuse is ringing in the theater," Ms. Darbus was saying. "What temerity! For the theater is a temple of art, a precious cornucopia of creative energy . . ."

Only Ryan and Sharpay were still listening. They nodded soberly in agreement.

Chad was now asleep inside the fake tree. He was even snoring.

Just as everyone thought they might faint from boredom, Coach Bolton ran into the auditorium, the light of battle shining in his eyes.

"Where's my team, Darbus?!" he yelled. "And what the heck are they doing here!?"

Ms. Darbus pulled herself to her full height and said icily, "It's called crime and punishment . . . Coach Bolton." She swept her arm toward the stage and added, "And proximity to the arts is cleansing for the soul."

Unfortunately, Chad chose that moment to suddenly wake up and fall out of his fake tree.

Coach Bolton held his temper and said to Ms. Darbus, as quietly as he could, "May we have a word?" He pointed to Troy and Chad and snapped, "You two, into the gym. Right now."

Troy and Chad jumped up, overjoyed at their

sudden release from prison. As they dashed for the door, Troy reached into the bucket and grabbed his cell phone.

And then they were gone. Gabriella had watched them the whole way.

Principal Matsui sat behind his desk, looking with resignation at the school's basketball coach and drama teacher. The coach was angry. The drama teacher was defiant. And Principal Matsui was starting to get that familiar feeling of heartburn. . . .

"If they have to paint sets for detention, they can do it tonight, not during my practice," the coach said.

Ms. Darbus appealed to the principal's sense of fair play. "If these were theater performers instead of athletes, would you seek special treatment?"

"Darbus, we are days away from the biggest game of the year," Coach Bolton said, exasperated.

"And we are in the midst of auditions for our winter musical, as well," the drama teacher shot back. "This school is about more than young men in baggy shorts flinging balls for touchdowns."

"Baskets," the coach said through gritted teeth. "They shoot baskets."

Principal Matsui sighed wearily. "Listen, guys, you've been having this argument since . . . let me think"—he raised his voice—"*since the day you both started teaching here!*" In a more reasonable tone, he added, "We are one school, one student body, one faculty. Can we not agree on that?"

The coach and drama teacher stared at him in disbelief. Clearly, they weren't going to agree on anything.

The principal shook his head and picked up a mini basketball from his desk. He tossed it toward the small basketball hoop on his wall and asked, "How's the team looking, anyway? Troy got them whipped into shape?"

Ms. Darbus could only roll her eyes.

**H**aving won his latest skirmish with Ms. Darbus, Coach Bolton returned to the gym. He paced in front of his team and reminded them of the sad truth they all knew. "The West High Knights have knocked us out of the playoffs three years running. Now we're one game away from taking the championship right back from them."

He stopped to look directly at each player in turn. "It's time to make our stand. The team is you, and you are the team. And the team doesn't exist unless each and every one of you is fully focused on our goal."

He focused on Troy and Chad, and added meaningfully, "Am I clear?"

They nodded as the whole team erupted into their cheer. "Wildcats! Getcha head in the game!"

Coach Bolton nodded, satisfied. They were pumped up. They were ready. And they were going to win!

Ms. Darbus's detention was over, and Taylor and Gabriella were finally free. As they walked across the courtyard together, Taylor said, "We've never made it out of the first round of the Scholastic Decathlon. You could be our answered prayer."

Gabriella smiled. She was flattered, but she didn't budge. "I'm going to focus on my studies this semester and help my mom get the new house organized. Maybe next year."

"But—" Taylor began.

Gabriella searched her mind for some way to change the subject, and immediately thought of a topic she was most curious about. "What do you know about Troy Bolton?"

"Troy?" Taylor raised her eyebrows in surprise. "I wouldn't consider myself an expert on that particular subspecies." Six cheerleaders were approaching them, walking in a pack, as usual. Taylor's eyes sparkled with mischief as she added, "However, unless you speak cheerleader, as in—" She put on an enthusiastic, cheerleader voice and said breathlessly, *"Isn't Troy Bolton just the hottie superbomb?"*

On cue, the cheerleaders nodded and squealed enthusiastically.

"See what I mean?" Taylor said to Gabriella.

Gabriella laughed. "I guess I wouldn't know how to speak cheerleader."

Taylor nodded, happy to have made her point. "Which is why we exist in an alternative universe to Troy-the-basketball-boy."

Gabriella nodded. She knew that Taylor was right. In every high school, there were the brainiacs, the jocks, the band kids, the cheerleaders, the slackers . . . And every group was its own clique. No one ever moved from one clique to another. No one.

Still . . .

"Have you tried to get to know him?" she asked.

Taylor just laughed. "Watch how it works in the cafeteria tomorrow when you have lunch with us. Unless you'd rather sit with the cheerleaders and discuss the importance of firm nail beds."

"My nail beds are history," Gabriella said, smiling as she held up her hands to illustrate her point.

Taylor laughed and held up her hands in turn. Her nails looked just as bad as Gabriella's. "Sister!" she cried, and they slapped hands in brainiac solidarity.

It was almost dark, but Troy was still in his backyard, shooting hoops. His father watched approvingly; his boy had moves, he thought. Good moves. Great moves, in fact.

He had to make sure Troy didn't lose focus. Not now.

"I still don't understand this detention thing," he said.

"It was my mess-up," Troy answered quickly, hoping this wouldn't turn into a big discussion. "Sorry, Dad."

"Darbus will grab any opportunity to bust my chops, and yours, too," his father reminded him.

Troy nodded, but his mind was on other things. After a moment, he asked hesitantly, "Dad, did you ever think about trying something new but were afraid of what your friends might think?

"You mean working on going left?" his dad asked. "You're doing fine."

Troy sighed but tried again. "I meant—what if you try something really new and it's a disaster, and all your friends laugh at you?"

"Then maybe they're not your friends," his father said. "That was my whole point about 'team' today. You guys have to look out for each other. And you're their leader."

"Yeah, but—" Troy was getting frustrated. He was really confused here, what with Gabriella and the musical and the way he had felt singing with her, and all his dad could think about was the basketball game.

"There are going to be college scouts at our game next week, Troy," his father said, as if Troy needed reminding. "Do you know what a scholarship is worth these days?"

"A lot?" Troy said. He didn't need to ask. He knew that a basketball scholarship could pay for four years of college. It would really help his parents financially. And it would help set him up for the future.

His father nodded. "Focus, Troy."

And Troy nodded in agreement. That's what he had to do. Focus. Concentrate on basketball. Don't think about anything else—not even singing.

*Especially* not singing.

# ♪ CHAPTER 5 ♪

The next morning, Troy entered his homeroom class. The first person he saw was Gabriella. He sneaked a peek at her and realized she was looking at him, too. They both smiled sheepishly and looked away as Ms. Darbus said sternly, "I expect we learned our homeroom manners yesterday, people, correct?"

Everyone nodded obediently.

"If not, we have dressing rooms that need painting," she warned. "Now, a few announcements. This morning during free period is your chance for musical auditions, both singles and pairs. I'll be in the theater until noon, for those bold enough to explore the wingspan of their latent creative spirit."

Behind Troy, Chad rolled his eyes at this and leaned forward to whisper, "What time is she due back on the mother ship?"

His buddies snickered. Troy smiled uncomfortably. As he sat through the rest of homeroom, he tried to focus. Basketball, he kept saying to himself. Keep your eye on the prize, Troy. Don't think about anything except basketball.

When Ms. Darbus released the class, everyone piled out into the hallway. Chad quickly caught up with Troy. "Hey, Troy . . . the whole team's hitting the gym during free period. What are you going to have us run?"

Troy looked shifty. "Can't make it. I've got to catch up on homework."

Chad did a double take. "What?! Hello, this is only the second day back, dude," he protested. "I'm not even behind yet, and I've been behind on homework since preschool."

Troy smiled and shrugged. "Catch you later," he said, then melted away in the crowd.

Chad looked after him, puzzled. "Homework?" he asked himself. "No way." He followed Troy, determined to figure out this mystery.

Chad would never make a good spy, Troy thought, catching a glimpse of his buddy out of the corner of his eye. He saw an open classroom door and quickly ducked inside. He saw Chad peer inside, and started talking to a couple of students as a cover. Then someone passing in the hall called out to Chad. As soon as Troy saw that his friend was distracted, he slipped out the back door of the classroom, scooted down the hall, and hurried down a stairwell.

The stairwell led outside to the courtyard. As Troy darted across the open area, he suddenly saw his father walking toward him. Thinking fast, Troy hid behind a wall, then opened the door to the automotive shop. He slipped inside just as his father approached.

Funny, Coach Bolton thought, I could have sworn I just saw Troy. . . . He looked around, but his son was nowhere in sight. The coach shrugged. I must be seeing things. Must be the pressure of the big game, he thought, and went on.

Troy's evasive skills and fast footwork came in handy as he moved quickly around the large pieces of equipment in the auto shop. As he reached the door, the auto-shop teacher approached.

". . . shortcut . . ." Troy explained quickly. ". . . late for class . . ." Then he ducked out the door, ran down the hall, and entered the school theater from the backstage.

He peered out through the stage curtains and saw dozens of kids arriving, eager to try out. He spotted the janitor's cart with a mop and bucket. He turned the mop upside down and used it as cover as he rolled the cart down a ramp, along the side of the theater and into the shadows at the back of the auditorium.

From his safe hiding place, he watched as Ms. Darbus stepped onto the stage and began the auditions in her trademark dramatic style.

"This is where the true expression of the artist is realized, where inner truth is revealed through the actor's journey, where—" She stopped suddenly to glare around the theater.

". . . WAS THAT A CELL PHONE?" she snapped.

Kelsi, the composer of this year's musical, was seated at a piano onstage. She answered Ms. Darbus timidly. "No, ma'am, it was the recess bell."

Ms. Darbus nodded, satisfied that her domain had not been invaded. "Those wishing to audition must understand that time is of the essence, we have many roles to cast, and the final callbacks will be next week. First, you'll sing a few bars, and then I will give you a sense of whether or not the theater is your calling. Better to hear it from me than from your friends. Our composer, Kelsi Neilsen, will accompany you, and be available for rehearsals prior to callbacks. Shall we?"

She took a seat in the front row and braced herself for what was to come. She had too many years of experience with student auditions. She knew it wasn't going to be pretty.

The first student, a shy boy with a slightly flat voice, took the stage. Kelsi began playing the audition song, "What I've Been Looking For," and he sang along. When they'd finished, Ms. Darbus thought that it hadn't been *horrible*, but it certainly wasn't up to her high standards. Next came

Susan, whose off-key voice and overly enthusiastic gestures were . . . well, Ms. Darbus thought, they were just scary bad. She winced as Susan belted out the song.

At the end of Susan's audition, Ms. Darbus put on a fake smile and said, "That's nice, Susan," adding, "perhaps best saved for a family gathering."

Then Alan bounded up, smiling. He was a very snappy dresser, but when he opened his mouth, Ms. Darbus realized sadly that he was a terrible singer.

She told him, "Alan, I admire your pluck. As to your voice . . . those are really nice shoes you're wearing. Next . . ."

Next was Cyndra, whose high-pitched wail made Ms. Darbus grimace. "Ah, Cyndra, what courage to pursue a note that's never been accessed in the natural world," she said, trying to be positive. "Bravo." She quickly corrected herself—after all, if there was one thing Ms. Darbus knew, it was theater terminology. *Bravo* was said to congratulate a male singer, while *brava* was said to a female. "Brava!" she said to Cyndra. "How about . . . the spring musical?

She thought she had reached her breaking point, but that was before she saw the next audition, a boy and a girl who made strange gestures and performed slow somersaults as they chanted the lyrics in a hypnotic monotone.

"Okay . . ." Ms. Darbus finally said. "That was . . . just plain disturbing. Go see a counselor."

As Troy watched the auditions wistfully, he felt a tap on his shoulder. It was Gabriella.

"Hey! You decided to sign up for something?" she asked.

"No," he answered. "You?"

She shook her head. "No." Then she took in his "disguise." "Why are you hiding behind a mop?"

Embarrassed, he awkwardly pushed the mop out of the way.

Gabriella looked at him knowingly. "Your friends don't know you're here, right?"

He hesitated, then admitted the truth. "Right." He glanced at the stage, where the auditions—and Ms. Darbus's putdowns—were continuing. "Ms. Darbus is a little . . . harsh."

"The Wildcat superstar is . . . afraid?" she teased him.

"Not afraid . . . just"—he hesitated again, then let his guard down—"scared."

Relieved, Gabriella said, "Me, too." She looked at Ms. Darbus, who was dismissing yet another hopeful singer. "Hugely."

As they nervously watched Ms. Darbus, the teacher checked her clipboard and announced, "For the lead roles of Arnold and Minnie, we only have one couple signed up." She smiled warmly at her star students. "Nevertheless, Ryan and Sharpay, I think it might be useful for you to give us a sense of why we gather in this hallowed hall."

This was just the moment Sharpay and Ryan were waiting for! They made grand entrances from opposite sides of the stage, and bowed to the almost-empty auditorium as if it were a Broadway theater filled with a cheering audience.

Sharpay glared at Kelsi, who jumped as she realized that she was expected to clap for them. Quickly regrouping, Kelsi asked shyly, "What key?" and prepared to play.

But Ryan lifted a boom box and said smugly, "We had our rehearsal pianist do an arrangement."

He hit the PLAY button, and he and his sister began their routine.

Their voices were great, Kelsi admitted to herself, and their dancing! They must have had a professional choreographer! But they had changed her soulful ballad into a fast, upbeat number. She couldn't help but feel disappointed as they sang.

They finished with a professional flourish and beamed proudly. They were good, and they knew they were good.

After that audition, everyone else knew it, too. The few kids who were gathering their courage to audition at the last minute quietly slinked out of the theater, totally intimidated.

"Don't be discouraged!" Ryan called after them. "The Drama Club doesn't just need singers, it needs fans, too! Buy tickets!"

Kelsi gathered her courage and approached Sharpay and Ryan. "Actually, if you do the part . . . with that particular song, I was hoping you'd—"

"*If* we do the part?" Sharpay interrupted her. "Kelsi, my sawed-off Sondheim, I've been in seventeen school productions. And how many times have *your* compositions been selected?"

"This is the first time," Kelsi admitted.

"Which tells us what?" Sharpay demanded.

Kelsi paused, not sure what answer was expected of her. "That I should write you more solos?"

Sharpay shook her head. "It tells us that you do *not* offer direction, suggestion, or commentary," she said condescendingly. "And you should be thankful that Ryan and I are here to lift your music out of its current obscurity. Are we clear?"

"Yes, ma'am," Kelsi said, thoroughly cowed. Then she caught herself. "I mean, Sharpay."

"Nice talking to you," Sharpay said in a tone of dismissal. She and Ryan turned on their heels and left with the regal stride of future superstars.

Kelsi began gathering her music, her pulse racing after this close encounter with celebrity ego.

"Okay, we're out of time, so if we have any last-minute sign-ups?" Ms. Darbus announced. She looked around the room. "No? Good. Done."

She tossed her clipboard into her shoulder bag and began to leave. Gabriella took a deep breath. It was now or never, she thought. Before she could have second thoughts, she ran up to the drama teacher.

"I'd like to audition, Ms. Darbus."

Ms. Darbus shook her head. "Timeliness means something in the world of theater, young lady. Plus, the individual auditions are long, long over. And there were simply no other pairs."

Then, out of the darkness, Troy's voice said, "I'll sing with her." He moved from the shadows to stand with Gabriella.

"Troy Bolton?" The drama teacher looked more than taken aback. She looked suspicious. "Where's your . . . sport posse, or whatever it's called?"

"Team," Troy said helpfully. "But I'm here alone. Actually"—he smiled at Gabriella—"I'm here to sing with her."

"Yes, well, we treat these shows very seriously here at East High," Ms. Darbus sniffed.

"I called for the pairs audition, and you didn't respond." She pointed to the clock. "Free period is over." Then, in an effort to sound gracious, she added, "Next musical, perhaps."

As she headed for the back of the auditorium, Kelsi started to leave the stage, clutching her sheet music. She was so distracted by all the drama—on and off the stage—that she tripped over the piano leg and sprawled to the floor. Her pages of music scattered everywhere.

Troy jumped up onstage, lifted her up, and began helping her collect the papers. Kelsi didn't lift a finger to help—she was too stunned. Troy Bolton, the Troy Bolton, the school's star basketball player, was helping her? She stared at him, frozen.

Troy didn't notice the effect he was having on Kelsi. "You composed the song that Ryan and Sharpay just sang?" he asked.

Speechless, Kelsi nodded.

"And the entire show?" he asked.

Again, Kelsi managed to nod. Barely.

"That's way cool," he said, truly impressed. "I can't wait to hear the rest of the show." When she didn't answer, he went on. "Why are you so afraid of Ryan and Sharpay? It's your show."

Kelsi was so startled, she actually blurted out a couple of words. "It is?"

"Isn't the composer of a show like the play-maker in basketball?" he asked.

"Playmaker?" Kelsi hadn't ever heard that term, but she liked the sound of it.

"The person who makes everyone else look good," he explained. "Without you, there *is* no show. You're the playmaker here, Kelsi."

"I am?" Kelsi had never thought of it that way before. But now that Troy Bolton—*the* Troy Bolton!—had said it, she had to admit, it made a certain kind of sense. Feeling bold and strong for the first time, she sat at the piano and asked, "Do you want to hear the way that duet is supposed to sound?"

She began playing the audition song that Ryan and Sharpay had rearranged. She played it more slowly, with feeling and soul. Troy and Gabriella listened with growing appreciation.

"Wow, now that's really nice," Troy said.

Kelsi pushed the music toward Troy.

He looked at it. Did he dare?

Gabiella looked at it, too, feeling tempted.

Then Troy began to sing softly:

*"It's hard to believe*
*That I couldn't see*
*You were always there beside me"*

Gabriella soon joined in, a little more boldly.

*"Thought I was alone*
*With no one to hold"*

When they sang together, the harmonies melded perfectly.

They both felt the same glow they had felt on New Year's Eve. Kelsi beamed as she listened to this simple, pure interpretation of her song. It was the way she had dreamed it would sound.

As they finished, Ms. Darbus stepped forward from the darkness by the back door. She had been watching and listening the entire time. And what she had seen and heard had surprised her.

As she wrote their names on her clipboard, she called out, "Bolton, Montez, you have a callback. Kelsi, give them the duet from the second act. Work on it with them."

The bell rang. Ms. Darbus strode off to her next

class as Troy and Gabriella looked at each other, totally stunned. Now what?

Kelsi handed them the music and said eagerly, "If you want to rehearse, I'm usually in the music room during free period and after school . . . and sometimes even during biology class."

All was quiet until the next morning. Then, Sharpay walked into school. She checked out the sheet that Ms. Darbus had posted, listing who had to take part in a second round of auditions. And she saw the dreaded phrase. . . .

"CALLBACK!!!" Her scream echoed through the halls of East High.

Ryan rushed to her side and read aloud from the sheet. "'Callback for roles of Arnold and Minnie, next Thursday, 3:30 P.M. Ryan and Sharpay Evans. Gabriella Montez and Troy Bolton.'"

"Is this some kind of joke?" Sharpay demanded angrily. "They didn't even audition."

"Maybe we're being punked?" Ryan suggested. "Maybe we're being filmed right now."

"Shut up, Ryan!" Sharpay snarled.

By this time, a crowd of students had gathered.

Troy's teammates Chad, Jason, and Zeke were among the students staring at the list.

Chad saw Troy's name. An expression of complete and utter horror crossed his face. "WHAT?!!!!!" he yelled.

By lunchtime, the news that Troy and Gabriella had tried out for the musical had spread throughout the school. As students entered the cafeteria, they took their usual seats. Jocks sat with jocks. Brainiacs sat with brainiacs. Drama kids sat with drama kids. Skater dudes, cheerleaders, punks . . . each sat with their own kind.

That was the way the world was meant to be. Orderly. Predictable. Understandable.

Sharpay held court at the head of the drama kids table. Kelsi sat at the far end, listening to every word, but keeping quiet, as usual.

"How dare she sign up," Sharpay said. "I've already picked out the colors for my dressing room."

"And she hasn't even asked our permission to join the Drama Club," Ryan pointed out supportively.

"Someone's got to tell her the rules," Sharpay decided.

"Exactly," her brother agreed. He thought for a moment, then asked, "What are the rules?"

As if he was just waiting for that cue, Zeke, a tall, burly basketball player with a killer smile, began singing. The other jocks gathered around, curious. Zeke looked at them, took a deep breath, and admitted, "If Troy admits he sings, then I can tell my secret." He whispered to them, "I bake."

"What?" Chad couldn't believe what he had heard.

But now that he had confessed, Zeke felt that he had been set free. "I love to bake," he said. "Scones, strudel, even apple pandowdy." He was too caught up in his enthusiasm to stop. "I dream of making the perfect crème brûlée," he said as Chad buried his face in his hands.

The jocks were horrified. Urgently, they sang:

*"No, no, no, noooooooooooooo*
*Stick to the stuff you know*
*If you wanna be cool*
*Follow one simple rule*

*Don't mess with the flow, no no*
*Stick to the status quo"*

Zeke had started something. Over at the brain-iacs table, Martha Cox, a studious girl who wore glasses and a plain skirt and sweater, suddenly jumped up from the table, threw her arms wide and exclaimed, "Hip-hop is my passion! I love to pop, lock, break, and jam."

She demonstrated a few moves, and one of the brainiac boys got worried. "Is that legal?" he asked the table.

Martha turned to the worried boy and said, "It's just . . . dancing. And the truth is, sometimes I think it's even cooler than"—she took a deep breath, gathered her courage, and finished—"homework!"

Her friends looked as if they were about to faint.

Meanwhile, across the cafeteria, a skateboarder stood up and confessed, "If Troy can be in a show, then I'm coming clean." He hesitated, then gave it up. "I play the cello."

"Awesome," said another skateboarder. "What is it?"

His friend mimed playing the cello, but saw only confusion in the other boarder's face.

"A saw?"

"No, it's like a giant violin," the first boarder explained.

"Do you have to wear a costume?" the second boarder asked.

"Tie and coat," the unmasked cello player said.

"That's uncalled for!" his friend exclaimed.

The spirit of rebellion was building, however! The skater dude jumped up on his table and enthusiastically mimed playing the cello. Brainiac Martha was busting out some cool hip-hop moves from the top of her table, dancing and swaying to the rhythm in her head.

The students who had confessed their secret loves were now all standing on their respective cafeteria tables as if they were on stages, singing their hearts out.

Finally, Sharpay had had enough! She shouted, "Everybody, quiet!" Her voice echoed through the room. All the students stopped and stared at Gabriella and Taylor, who had just entered the cafeteria and picked up their lunch trays.

Gabriella noticed the attention and said nervously, "Why are they pointing at you?"

"Not me," Taylor replied. "You."

"Because of the callback?" The memory of that horrible church choir experience flooded back into Gabriella's mind. "I can't have people stare at me. I really can't."

As Gabriella and Taylor wove through the crowd to a table, Gabriella stumbled. Her tray went flying and spilled chili fries, ketchup, and melted cheese all over . . . Sharpay.

Sharpay stood still, stone-faced, and Gabriella tried to clean the food from Sharpay's blouse. It only made the mess worse.

At that moment, Troy entered the cafeteria and noticed what was going on. He headed over to help Gabriella, but Chad quickly intercepted him. "You can't get in the middle of that, Troy," his buddy warned. "Far too dangerous."

He dragged Troy over to the safest place in the room: their usual table. Troy looked around and realized that the cafeteria was buzzing with energy and excitement.

"What's up?" he asked.

"Oh, let's see," Chad answered. "You missed free-period workout yesterday to audition for some heinous musical. Suddenly people are . . . confessing. Zeke is baking . . . crème brûlée."

Troy frowned, trying to follow all this. This was a lot of confusing information, so he seized on the easiest point to clear up. Crème brûlée?

"What's that?"

"A creamy, custardlike filling with a caramelized surface," Zeke said, happy to finally be able to talk about his secret passion. "Very satisfying."

Chad rolled his eyes. This was getting out of control! "Shut up, Zeke!" he yelled. Then he turned to Troy. "Do you see what's happening? Our team is coming apart because of your singing thing. Even the drama geeks and brainiacs suddenly think they can . . . talk to us. The skater dudes are . . . mingling. People think they can suddenly . . . do other stuff! Stuff that's . . . *not their stuff*!"

He pointed dramatically to the kids sitting at Sharpay's table. "They've got you thinking about show tunes when *we've* got a playoff game next week!"

At this moment, Ms. Darbus walked into the cafeteria and noted the unusual sense of turmoil among the students. She spotted Sharpay, who was trying, without success, to clean her blouse with a napkin.

"What happened here?" Ms. Darbus demanded.

"Look at this!" Sharpay cried indignantly. "That Gabriella girl dumped her lunch on me . . . on purpose! It's all part of their plan to ruin our musical."

She pointed an accusing finger at the jock table. "And Troy and his basketball robots are obviously behind it. Why do you think he auditioned?"

She sensed that she was convincing Ms. Darbus that some sort of conspiracy was being hatched. She smiled a bit and went on smoothly, "After all the work you've put into this show, it just doesn't seem right."

Kelsi watched and listened as Sharpay worked on Ms. Darbus. But despite her new confidence, she still couldn't take on the queen of the Drama Club *and* Ms. Darbus.

At least, not yet.

Coach Bolton was eating a sandwich at his desk and reading the newspaper sports page when Ms. Darbus suddenly barged in. He dropped the paper with a sigh—he had been having such a nice, peaceful lunch—as the drama teacher said, "All right, Bolton, cards on the table right now."

"Huh?" Sometimes Coach Bolton thought that all that make-believe was affecting Ms. Darbus's mind. She always seemed off in some other world, from what he could see.

"You're tweaked that I put your stars in detention, so now you're getting even?" Ms. Darbus was beside herself with rage.

"What are you talking about, Darbus?" The coach was honestly confused.

"Your 'all-star' son turned up for my audition," Ms. Darbus said. "I give every student an even chance, which is the long and honorable tradition of the theater—something you wouldn't understand—but if he's planning some kind of practical joke in my chapel of the arts—"

The coach grasped the one truth he knew he

could cling to amid this barrage of nonsense. "Troy doesn't even sing."

"Oh, you're wrong about that. But I won't allow my *Twinkle Town* musical made into a farce—"

He could help it. He almost laughed in her face, but managed to choke it back at the last second. "*Twinkle Town?*" he asked.

Apparently, his poker face wasn't as good as he thought. Ms. Darbus knew he was laughing, and immediately assumed that he had sent Troy to audition as some kind of practical joke.

"See!" she cried. "I knew it! I knew it!"

Back in the cafeteria, Taylor and Gabriella were still trying to recover from the chaos that had erupted.

"Is Sharpay really, really mad?" Gabriella asked. "I said I was sorry."

"No one has beaten out Sharpay for a musical since kindergarten," Taylor explained.

"I'm not trying to beat anyone out," Gabriella protested. "We weren't even auditioning. We were just . . . singing."

Taylor shook her head. "You won't convince

Sharpay of that," she warned. "If that girl could figure out how to play both Romeo and Juliet, her own brother would be aced out of a job."

"I told you, it just . . . happened." Then she admitted the real truth. "But . . . I liked it. A lot."

She sighed and then asked Taylor the question she had been wondering about ever since New Year's Eve. "Do you ever feel like there's this whole other person inside of you, just looking for a way to come out?"

Taylor gave her a sharp look. "No," she said decisively.

The bell rang to signal the end of the lunch period. Sharpay stalked out of the cafeteria, but not before leveling a death-ray glance at Gabriella.

Then Zeke stepped up to stop Sharpay. He was fizzing with happiness now that his secret love of baking was out in the open.

"Hey, Sharpay," he said. "Now that Troy's going to be in your show . . ."

"Troy Bolton is *not* in my show!" she snapped.

Zeke pushed on, undeterred. "I thought maybe you'd like to come to see me play ball sometime. . . ."

Sharpay tossed her head and said grandly, "I'd rather stick pins in my eyes."

He frowned at her, puzzled. "Wouldn't that be awfully uncomfortable?"

She rolled her eyes in exasperation. "Evaporate, tall person!" she said as she stormed away.

Crestfallen, Zeke called after her, "I bake . . . if that helps."

The next day, Gabriella opened her locker and found a note. She read it quickly, then looked at a yellow door at the end of the hall. She was a little confused—and very intrigued.

She opened the door and found a staircase that led up to the roof. As she opened the door and stepped out into the beautiful, sunny day, she saw Troy sitting on a bench. He was surrounded by lush plants, all being grown as hydroponic experiments.

"So this is your private hideout?" she asked, smiling.

"Thanks to the Science Club," Troy said. "Which means my buddies don't even know about it."

Gabriella wondered about that. His teammates didn't seem to be his only buddies.

"Looks to me like everyone on campus wants to be your friend," she pointed out.

"Unless we lose."

He seemed a little down about that, she thought. The pressure must be intense, especially since . . .

"I'm sure it's tricky being the coach's son," she said.

Troy shrugged. "It makes me practice a little harder, I guess. I don't know what he'll say when he hears about the singing thing."

"You're worried?" She was surprised. Troy seemed so cool, so confident. Not the type to worry. Ever.

But Troy nodded. "My parents' friends are always saying, 'Your son is the basketball guy, you must be so proud.' Sometimes I don't want to be the basketball guy. I just want to be . . . a guy."

Gabriella smiled with understanding. He didn't want to be the basketball guy any more than she wanted to be genius girl. They were both so much more than that. . . .

"I saw how you treated Kelsi at the audition yesterday," she said softly. "Do your friends know *that* guy?"

He shook his head. "To them, I'm the play-maker dude."

"Then they don't know enough about you, Troy." Gabriella paused, then decided it was time to share a confession of her own. "At my other schools I was the freaky math girl. It's cool coming here and being . . . anyone I want to be. When I was singing with you, I just felt like . . . a girl."

"You even looked like one, too," he teased her.

She laughed, glad to have the seriousness of the moment lightened a bit. "Remember in kindergarten you'd meet a kid, know nothing about them, then ten seconds later were best friends, because you didn't have to be anything but yourself?"

"Yeah . . ." Troy's voice was wistful.

"Singing with you felt like that," Gabriella said sincerely.

"I never thought about singing, that's for sure," Troy said. "Until you."

"So you really want to do the callbacks?" she asked.

He thought about it for a moment as he looked at her. Really looked at her. Then he smiled. "Hey, just call me freaky callback boy."

She smiled, a glowing smile of pure happiness. "You're a cool guy, Troy. But not for the reasons your friends think." He looked down, a little embarrassed, and she moved on quickly. "Thanks for showing me your top secret hiding place. Like kindergarten."

Then the bell rang, breaking the mood and making Troy realize he was late. And that meant detention!

The next day, Kelsi sat alone at the piano, playing with passion and energy. No one else was in the room. Just Kelsi and her music. Exactly the way she liked it.

Troy sat in a stairwell, practicing his audition song. He kind of liked the way his voice echoed.

At that moment, Ryan rounded a corner and slowed down to listen. He could have sworn he heard someone singing. . . .

Meanwhile, Gabriella had found her own private spot with great acoustics: the girls' bathroom.

She stood in front of the mirror and sang.

Sharpay was heading for class when she thought she heard the faint sound of singing. She turned her head to spot where it was coming from . . . there! She opened the bathroom door and went in, looking everywhere for the source of the music.

She found . . . nothing.

I've been rehearsing too much, Sharpay thought as she left the bathroom. I'm starting to hear that music everywhere I go!

Gabriella stepped out of the hiding place she had quickly found for herself and smiled.

Later that day, in the school's rehearsal room, Kelsi played the piano for Gabriella and helped her with her phrasing.

Then it was Troy's turn. He worked as hard as he could, but singing was harder than he thought. Just when he was getting frustrated beyond belief, Kelsi would stop to encourage him.

Just like basketball, he thought. You've gotta keep practicing.

And he started to sing again.

★ ☆ ★

**T**he other basketball players were in the gym, warming up for practice. Coach Bolton kept checking his watch. Where was Troy? He frowned. Something was going on with that boy. Something weird. Something different. And it was getting in the way of his championship dream.

Coach Bolton didn't like it. He didn't like it at all.

He would have liked it even less if he had known where Troy was.

In detention. Again.

The only bright side was that Gabriella was there, too. They stole glances at each other as they painted scenery. Each one was smiling a secret smile. Each one was hearing the audition song in their heads.

Finally, detention was over. Troy raced into the gym—only to find that practice was over, too.

The players headed toward the locker room. Hoping to recover a bit from his absence, Troy said to his father, "I'm going to stay awhile, work on free throws."

Coach Bolton nodded coldly in agreement. "Since you were late for practice . . . again . . . I think your teammates deserve a little extra effort from you."

He gave Troy a hard look, then headed for his office.

Troy sighed. He started shooting baskets, sinking one after the other.

Then Gabriella poked her head around the door. He smiled in welcome and waved her in.

She entered cautiously, looking around with curiosity. "Wow, so this is your . . . real stage."

"I guess you could call it that," he said. "Or just a smelly gym."

He bounced the ball over to her. She grabbed it and took a shot. It went in, and Troy turned to her, surprised.

"Whoa . . . don't tell me you're good at hoops, too?"

"I once scored forty-one points in a league championship game," she said, straight-faced.

"No way," he said, impressed.

"Yeah," she laughed, "the same day I invented the space shuttle and microwave popcorn."

He laughed, stole the ball back from her, took a shot, and missed. She grabbed it on the rebound and said, "I've been rehearsing with Kelsi."

"I know," he said. "Me, too. And I was late for practice. So if I get kicked off the team, it'll be on your conscience."

Gabriella looked startled. "Hey, I—"

"Gabriella," Troy said, laughing. "Chill."

She gave him a stern look for the teasing just as Coach Bolton came back to the gym.

"Miss, I'm sorry, this is a closed practice," the coach said, his voice booming in the empty gym.

"Dad, practice is over," Troy protested.

"Not until the last player leaves the gym," the coach said. "Team rules."

Gabriella sensed the tension between them and quickly said, "Oh, I'm sorry, sir."

"Dad, this is Gabriella Montez," Troy said.

Gabriella looked at the coach with interest. So this was Troy's father. . . .

The coach looked at her with disapproval. "Your detention buddy?" he said.

Okay. Gabriella knew when it was time to

leave. "I'll see you later, Troy," she said. "Nice to meet you, Coach Bolton."

"You as well, Miss Montez," the coach said, as he gave her a stern look.

Troy faced his dad. "Detention was my fault, not hers."

"You haven't missed practice in three years," his father pointed out. "That girl turns up and you're late twice."

Troy felt anger flare up in his chest. "'That girl' is named Gabriella, and she's very nice," he said sharply.

"Helping you miss practice doesn't make her 'very nice,'" his dad said, just as sharply. "Not in my book. Or your team's."

"She's not a problem, Dad," Troy said, frustrated. Why was his father—why was his coach—making such a big deal about this? "She's just . . . a girl."

"But you're not just 'a guy,' Troy." His father—and his coach—was equally frustrated. "You're the team leader, so what you do affects not only this team, but the entire school. Without you completely focused, we won't win the game next week. And playoff games don't come along all the time . . . they're something special."

Without warning, a series of memories ran through Troy's mind: Singing with Gabriella. Laughing with Gabriella. Talking with Gabriella.

"A lot of things are special," he said.

"You're a playmaker, not a singer," his father reminded him.

Exasperated, Troy yelled, "Did you ever think maybe I could be both?" He turned abruptly and headed for the locker room.

His dad watched him go, worried. He hoped he had been able to get through to Troy, but he feared that he hadn't.

Inside the hall between the locker room and the gym, Chad, Jason, and Zeke huddled together. They had been listening, wide-eyed, to the confrontation between Troy and his father.

Now they looked at one another and shook their heads.

This was not good. This was not good at all.

# CHAPTER 6

The next day, Chad sat next to Troy at a study table in the library. Without even saying hello, he started right in with the question on his mind—not to mention the minds of everyone on the team.

"What spell has this elevated-IQ temptress-girl cast that suddenly makes you want to be in a musical?" he asked.

"I just . . . did it," Troy sighed. "Who cares?"

"Who cares?" Chad looked injured. "How about your most loyal best friend?"

The librarian glared at him. "Quiet in here, Mr. Danforth."

Chad pointed at Troy. "It's him, Miss Falstaff, not me." Chad turned back to Troy, his voice more urgent now. "You're a hoops dude, not a musical-singer person. Have you ever seen Michael Crawford on a cereal box?"

"Who is Michael Crawford?" Troy asked.

"Exactly my point," Chad said, vindicated. "He was the Phantom of the Opera on Broadway. My mom saw that musical twenty-seven times and put Michael Crawford's picture in our refrigerator. Not on it, *in* it. Play basketball, you end up on a cereal box. Sing in musicals, you end up inside my mom's refrigerator."

Troy frowned, trying to follow this logic. "Why did she put his picture in her refrigerator?"

"One of her crazy diet ideas," he said dismissively. "I do not attempt to understand the female mind, Troy. That's frightening territory."

He looked up to see the librarian heading in their direction. He leaned over and whispered, "How can you expect the rest of us to be focused on the game if you're off somewhere in leotards singing in *Twinkle Town*?"

"No one said anything about leotards. . . ." Troy sounded a little worried.

Chad seized his advantage. "Maybe not yet, my friend, but just wait! We need you, Captain. Big-time."

Oops. The librarian was looming over them. "Mr. Danforth!"

Chad pointed to Troy again. "I tried to tell him, Miss Falstaff!" he said, the picture of innocence. To further the illusion, he turned to Troy and added, "I really tried!"

Then he crept away, followed by the librarian's accusing glare. Troy sat very still, thinking hard about what Chad had said.

**I**nside the chemistry lab, Taylor and the other members of the Scholastic Club were hard at work when Chad, Jason, and Zeke entered.

Chad walked up to Taylor and said, "We need to talk."

The two groups were deep in conversation when Sharpay and Ryan passed the open door of the chemistry lab. They stopped to look and listen.

"Something isn't right," Sharpay said.

Ryan nodded. "They must be trying to figure out a way for Troy and Gabriella to actually beat us out. The jocks rule most of the school, but if they get Troy into the musical, then they've conquered the entire student body."

"And if those science girls get Gabriella hooked up with Troy Bolton, the Scholastic Club goes from drool to cool," Sharpay gasped. Her eyes narrowed. "Ryan, we need to save our show from people who don't know the difference between a Tony Award and Tony Hawk."

Back in the chemistry lab, Chad had finished making his pitch to Taylor and her team.

"You really think that's going to work?" Taylor asked. The other members of the Scholastic Club looked equally dubious.

"It's the only way to save Troy and Gabriella from themselves," Chad said with certainty.

Taylor looked at her team for their input. After a brief pause, they all nodded. After all, they needed Gabriella as much as the basketball team needed Troy.

"We start tomorrow," Chad said, satisfied.

The next morning, as students poured into the school, Chad looked around secretively, as if on a spy mission. He spotted Taylor across the courtyard and gave a quick nod, in the best secret agent style.

She rolled her eyes at his theatrics and met him in a corner.

"My watch says seven forty-five, mountain standard time," he said in a hushed tone. "Are we synched?"

Taylor never wore a watch. She had an infallible inner clock. "Whatever."

"Then we are on go mode for lunch period?" Chad asked. "Exactly 12:05?"

She nodded and handed him a small laptop with a video lens attached. "Yes, Chad," she said. "We're a go. But we're not Charlie's Angels, okay?"

He grinned. "I can dream, can't I?"

And they were off.

At exactly 12:05, the lunch bell rang. Dozens of students headed to the cafeteria for lunch, but Troy headed for the locker room.

He arrived to find his whole team waiting for him. As he stepped in the room, Jason closed the door behind him and stood in front of it, blocking it with his body.

Chad stood in the center of the room next to a table covered with trophies and photos. He picked up one of the photos and held it up for Troy to see.

"'Spider' Bill Natrine, class of '99," Chad said. "MVP, league championship game."

He pointed to a trophy from that game.

Zeke held up the next photo.

"Sam Netletter, class of '02," he said. "Known far and wide as 'Sammy Slamma-Jamma.' Captain, MVP, league championship team."

He pointed to that trophy as Jason picked up the next photo.

"'Thunderclap' Hap Haddon, '95," Jason said, and pointed to the relevant trophy. "Led the Wildcats to back-to-back city championships. A legend."

"Yes, legends, one and all," Chad said, underlining the theme. "And do you think any of these Wildcat legends *became* legends by getting involved in musical auditions, just days before the league championship *playoffs*?"

The team stared intently at Troy and chanted in unison, "Getcha head in the game!"

"These Wildcat legends became legends because they never took their eye off the prize," Chad said. He was on a roll.

The team chanted again. "Getcha head in the game!"

Chad turned to the team and asked, "Now, who was the first sophomore ever to make starting varsity?"

The team smiled as one. "Troy!" they yelled.

Chad nodded. "So who voted him our team captain for *this* year?"

"Us!" the team yelled.

"And who is going to get their sorry butts

kicked in Friday's championship game if Troy is worried about an audition?" Chad asked.

"We are," the team said together, depressed.

"Hey, there are twelve of us on this team," Troy protested. "Not just me."

Chad raised one eyebrow. "Just twelve? I think you're forgetting a very important thirteenth member of this squad—" He pulled out another photo.

It was a black-and-white photo of a kid in a basketball uniform. From the style of the uniform—and the style of the hair—it was clear this photo was old-school.

Troy took a good look. His jaw dropped. "That's my dad . . ." he whispered.

Chad propped the photo against an old trophy. "Yes, Troy, Wildcat basketball champion, class of 1981. Champion . . . father—and now coach. A winning tradition like no other."

Troy looked around at his team. What was going on? He felt as if his team was trying to deprogram him or something!

Meanwhile, Gabriella and the rest of the Scholastic Club had gathered in the chemistry lab with brown-bag lunches. Taylor was pointing to a series of photos and sketches on the dry-erase board. They showed the process of evolution, Taylor style.

She lectured, "From lowly Neanderthal and Cro-Magnon, to early warriors, medieval knights . . . all leading to"—she unscrolled the pièce de résistance, a full-length photo of an NBA player's body, with Troy's head superimposed on it—"lunkhead basketball man! Yes, our culture worshipped the aggressor throughout the ages, and we end up with spoiled, overpaid, bonehead athletes who contribute little to civilization other than slam dunks and touchdowns. That is the inevitable world of Troy Bolton."

Gabriella smiled, not knowing what was coming.

Taylor went to another wall, saying, "But the path of the mind, the path we are on . . . ours is the path that has brought the world *these* people—"

She pointed to photos as she called out each name. "Eleanor Roosevelt . . . Frida Kahlo . . .

Sandra Day O'Connor . . . Madame Curie . . . Jane Goodall . . . Oprah Winfrey, and so many others who the world reveres."

Gabriella nodded. There was no doubt those were admirable people. "But . . . what has this . . . I've got Kelsi waiting for me to rehearse. . . ."

"Gabriella, Troy Bolton represents one side of evolution . . . lunkhead basketball man," Taylor explained patiently. "And our side, the side of education and accomplishment, is the future of civilization. That's the side where you belong."

In the locker room, Troy was doing his best to defend himself to his team. "If you guys don't know that I'll put one hundred and ten percent of my guts into that game, then you don't know *me*."

"Well, we just thought—" Chad began.

"I'll tell you what *I* thought," Troy said. "I thought you were my friends—win together, lose together . . . teammates."

Chad tried to explain their side of the story. "But suddenly the girl and the singing—" He was standing next to Taylor's laptop with the video-link camera.

Troy sighed, tired of discussing this and tired of

defending himself. "I'm for the team, I've always been for the team. She's just someone I met. . . ."

Troy didn't know it, but the laptop camera was transmitting the live feed of everything he was saying to the chemistry lab . . .

. . . where Gabriella, Taylor, and the rest of the Scholastic Club watched what Troy was saying.

". . . The singing thing is nothing, probably just a way to keep my nerves down, it doesn't mean anything to me," Troy was saying. "You're my guys and this is our team . . . Gabriella's not important. I'll forget the audition, forget her, and we'll go get that championship. Everyone happy now?"

Taylor froze the image on the screen. "Behold," she said. "Lunkhead basketball man. So, Gabriella . . . we'd love to have you for the Scholastic Decathlon."

Gabriella stared at the screen, crushed by what Troy said. They had shared so much—surely it had meant *something* to him?

The other girls awkwardly shuffled toward the door. No one looked at Gabriella. On her way out, Taylor said, "Do you want to grab some lunch?"

Gabriella shook her head. She just wanted to be alone.

Taylor nodded and left.

Just then, Gabriella heard noise from the quad below. She went to the window and looked out in time to see an impromptu pep rally. The basketball team was swarming around Troy, trying to pump him up for the big game.

Gabriella felt so sad, so alone. And, just as she had been doing since New Year's Eve, she started to express herself in song:

*"It's funny when you find yourself*
*Looking from the outside*
*I'm standing here*
*But all I want is to be over there*
*Why did I let myself believe*
*Miracles could happen*
*'Cause now I have to pretend*
*That I don't really care"*

She left the chemistry lab. The halls of East High were filled with trophy cases, banners, and murals. All she wanted was to get away from Wildcat spirit, and it was impossible.

She finally got to her locker. As she began putting books into it, Troy came up to her. He was beaming, filled with energy and high spirits from the pep rally.

"Hey, how ya doin'?" he called.

She didn't look at him.

"Listen, there's something I need to talk to you about, okay?" he went on.

"And here it is," she interrupted him. "I know what it's like to carry the load with friends. I get it. You've got your boys, Troy. It's okay. So we're good."

"Good about what?" he asked, puzzled. "I need to talk to you about the final callbacks."

She tried to smile. It was better if she ended this now, rather than let him do it. She could act like it was all her own idea. At least, she thought, I'll still have my pride. . . .

"I don't want to do the callbacks, either," she said quickly. "Who were we kidding? You've got your team, and now I've got my team. I'll do the Scholastic Decathlon, you win your championship.

It's where we belong." She smiled bravely. "Go, Wildcats."

Now Troy was the one who was bewildered and hurt. "But I don't—"

Gabriella didn't let him finish. "Me either," she said firmly.

She pulled the sheet music from her locker, handed it to him, and walked away.

"Gabriella!" Troy called.

She didn't respond. The bell rang, signaling the start of the next class.

Troy stared after her, stunned and hurt.

# CHAPTER 7

Over the next few days, Gabriella and Troy became more and more depressed. Gabriella thought Troy had dumped her. Troy thought Gabriella had dumped him. And, even though their friends tried to cheer them up, nothing worked.

One day, during PE class, Chad, Jason, Zeke, and some other students were goofing around on the outside basketball court. They were passing a ball in a circle, fast and slick, just like the Harlem Globetrotters. Laughing, they waved at Troy, inviting him to join them.

But Troy ignored them and headed over to the track for a jog instead, moving steadily away from his friends.

That evening, Troy shot baskets alone in his backyard. He missed a few baskets and slammed the ball down in frustration. His father watched from an upstairs window, worried. He knew something was wrong. He also knew it wasn't the right time to try to find out what it was.

At the Montez house, Gabriella was sitting by her bedroom window. She was surrounded by her books, but she wasn't reading. Instead, she was gazing out the window at the stars and trying not to cry.

Her mother opened the door, holding a portable phone. She held it out to Gabriella, indicating that the call was for her.

Gabriella just shook her head.

The next day, Gabriella and Troy happened to pass each other in the cafeteria. They glanced at each other, then away . . . then defused the awkward moment by moving on without saying a word.

Chad and Taylor saw the exchange from opposite ends of the room. They looked at each other and nodded. They'd seen enough. They could see the effect of what they'd done, and they knew that they'd screwed up, big-time.

Now they had to try to fix it. . . .

Troy was sitting by himself in the rooftop garden, glumly eating a sandwich. The door opened and Chad, Zeke, and Jason appeared.

"We just had another team meeting, Troy," Chad said.

"Wonderful," Troy answered. He tried to keep the bitterness out of his voice.

Chad swallowed hard. "We had a meeting about how we haven't been acting like a team. Us, not you. The singing thing—"

"I don't want to talk about it," Troy said shortly.

"We just want you to know that we're going to be there cheering for you," Chad finished.

Troy looked up, surprised. "Huh?"

Zeke nodded furiously. "Yeah, Cap, if singing is

something you want to do, we should be boosting you up, not tearing you down."

"Win or lose, we're teammates," Chad added. "That's what we're about. Even if you turn out to be the worst singer in the world—"

"—which we don't know, because we haven't actually heard you sing," Jason pointed out.

Troy sighed. It was great to finally have the support of his buddies, but it didn't mean anything anymore. "And you're not gonna hear me sing, dudes, because Gabriella won't even to talk to me, and I don't know why."

Chad and the boys exchanged uneasy glances. "We do," Chad finally said.

Zeke pulled a bag of cookies from his backpack and offered them to Troy. "Baked these fresh today. Want to try one before we tell you the rest?"

Inside the chemistry lab, Gabriella was surrounded by Taylor and the Scholastic Club.

"We're worse than jerks," Taylor was saying earnestly, "because we're mean jerks. We thought Troy Bolton and the singing thing was killing our chances to have you on our Scholastic Decathlon team."

"Why talk about it?" Gabriella said curtly. "I heard what he had to say. I'm on your team now. Done."

"No," Taylor sighed. "Not done." She hesitated, then admitted, "Chad knew he could get Troy to say things that would make you want to forget about the callbacks. We planned it. And we're embarrassed and sorry."

Gabriella absorbed the shock of that, but she said, "No one forced Troy to say anything." She took a deep breath and went on bravely. "And you know what? It's okay. We should be preparing for the decathlon now. So it's time to move on."

Taylor shook her head. She couldn't let this defeatist attitude go unchallenged. "No, it's not," she said in ringing tones. "The Scholastic Decathlon is . . . whatever. How you feel about us, and Troy, that's something else."

That evening, Mrs. Montez opened the front door to find Troy Bolton standing on her doorstep.

"Mrs. Montez, I'm Troy Bolton," he said politely.

Her eyes widened a little. So this was the Troy she had heard about from Gabriella! She smiled. "Oh . . . Troy . . ."

She glanced over her shoulder. Gabriella was standing on the stairs, just out of Troy's line of sight. She shook her head adamantly.

Mrs. Montez raised one eyebrow, but she got the message. She turned back to Troy and said, "Well, Gabriella is a little busy with homework and such, so now's not really a good time. . . ."

"I made a mistake, Mrs. Montez, and I need to let Gabriella know that," he said in a rush. "Could you tell her that I came by to see her?"

She nodded and smiled as she closed the door. Troy Bolton, she thought. He certainly seems like a nice boy. . . .

As Troy left, he crossed the lawn and glanced up. He saw a light go on at the far end of the second story. There was a small balcony outside the window. Suddenly inspired, Troy took out his cell phone and dialed Gabriella's number.

In her room, Gabriella saw Troy's photo come up on her cell phone screen. After a long moment, she answered.

As soon as he heard her voice, Troy said in a rush, "What you heard the other day . . . none of that is true. I was sick of my friends riding me about singing with you, and I said things I knew would shut them up. I didn't mean any of it."

"You sounded pretty convincing to me," she said coolly.

Troy looked up. He could see Gabriella walking around in her room. He looked up at the balcony for a moment, then he looked at a nearby tree. Then he started climbing.

As he climbed, he continued to talk into the phone. "The guy you met on vacation is way more me than the guy who said those stupid things."

"Troy, the whole singing thing is making the school act insane," Gabriella sighed. "You said it yourself, everyone is treating you different because of it."

Troy grabbed a branch and pulled himself a few feet higher. "Maybe that's because I don't want only to be the basketball guy anymore," he argued. "They can't handle it. That's not my problem, it's theirs."

He pulled himself up onto the balcony. Gabriella

was only a few feet away, but her back was to him. She didn't know he was there.

She said, "But your dad—"

"This isn't about my dad," he said, still talking into the phone. "This is about how I feel. And I'm not letting the team down. . . . They let me down. I'm going to sing. What about you?"

"I don't know, Troy."

"You need to say yes," he said. "Because I brought something for you."

Gabriella looked confused. "What do you mean?"

Troy lowered his phone and began to sing to her, directly, sweetly, honestly.

*"Start of something new*
*It feels so right*
*To be here with you . . . oh*
*And now . . . lookin' in your eyes*
*I feel in my heart*
*The start of something new"*

Gabriella turned around to see Troy standing on the balcony outside her room.

"It's a *pairs* audition," he reminded her. Then he handed her the sheet music she had given back to him. After a long shared look, Gabriella began to smile.

The next few days were a whirlwind of activity for both of them. Troy led basketball practices with energy and authority, back on top of his game. Gabriella ran through formulas with the Scholastic Club, more focused and impressive than they had ever seen her. Then they would run out of their separate practices, meet in the hall, and dash for the rehearsal room to rehearse with Kelsi.

One day, Sharpay and Ryan came out of their own rehearsal and heard Gabriella and Troy singing.

"Wow, they sound good," Ryan said.

Sharpay turned on him. "We have to do something. Our callback is on Thursday, the basketball game and Scholastic Decathlon are on Friday." She stopped. An idea—a good idea, possibly a great idea—was forming. "Too bad all of these events aren't happening on the same day at the same time."

"Well, that wouldn't work," Ryan said with his

104

usual naïveté, "because then Troy and Gabriella couldn't make the callback."

Sharpay gave him a look and waited for the implications to sink into her brother's dim brain.

Finally, his face lit up and he said, "I'm proud to call you my sister."

Later, Sharpay and Ryan cornered Ms. Darbus and spent some minutes talking earnestly to her.

Finally, Ms. Darbus said, "So if you're telling me, as copresidents of the Drama Club, that changing the callbacks is what's best for our theater program . . . I might actually agree with you."

She walked away. Ryan scratched his head.

"Was that a yes?" he asked his sister.

She gave him a wink that said, "Mission accomplished."

What they didn't notice—because they never noticed Kelsi—was that the shy young composer was standing nearby and had witnessed the entire thing.

Including the wink.

★ ☆ ★

The next morning, Troy and Gabriella got to school early so they could meet Kelsi and work in a little more rehearsal. They found her standing in front of the bulletin board, her face ashen.

The sign on the board said: MUSICAL AUDITIONS RESCHEDULED TO FRIDAY 3:30 P.M.

Troy and Gabriella stared glumly at those fatal words.

"Same time as the game—" Troy said.

"And the Scholastic Decathlon—" Gabriella added.

Chad and Taylor—accompanied, as always, by the basketball team and the Scholastic Club—gathered behind Troy and Gabriella.

"Well, I just don't know why they would do that," Taylor said, honestly puzzled.

"I smell a rat named Darbus," Chad said darkly.

"Actually, I think it's two rats, neither of them named Darbus," Kelsi said.

Everyone turned to see who had spoken. It took a minute—the petite Kelsi was almost lost among all the basketball players who towered over her.

"Do you know something about this, small person?" Chad asked.

Kelsi nodded. "Ms. Darbus might think she's protecting the show, but Ryan and Sharpay are pretty much only concerned with protecting themselves."

Chad's face tightened with anger. "Do you know what I'm going to do to those two over-coiffed show dogs—"

"Nothing," Troy said quickly, taking command. "We're not going to do anything to them." He grinned. "Except sing, maybe."

Troy looked at each member of the basketball team and Scholastic Club. "This is only going to happen if we all work together," he said. "Who's in?"

The teams eyeballed each other. Then Chad held up a hand. Taylor high-fived it. Everyone broke out into grins.

They were in.

On the day of the callback auditions, basketball championship game, and Scholastic Decathlon showdown, emotions were running high.

To demonstrate their newfound sense of solidarity, Chad and the basketball boys presented Taylor with a cake that Zeke had baked. The icing read: "Scholastic Decathlon Today—Support Brain Fame!"

In return, Taylor and her girls handed Chad a banner that read: "Go Wildcat Hoopsters!"

Ms. Darbus watched them sardonically. How lovely, she thought. The basketball boys and the brainiac girls are making nice. . . .

Then Chad and the boys walked up to Sharpay and Ryan and zipped open their jackets. Each one had a letter on his T-shirt, spelling out the message: "Go, Drama Club!"

Chad gave Sharpay a huge smile.

Ms. Darbus looked around at the banner, the cake, the boys with letter T-shirts, and smiled in spite of herself.

"Well, it seems we Wildcats are in for an interesting afternoon," she said drily. But her eyes were twinkling.

# ♪ CHAPTER 8 ♪

At three o'clock, the halls of East High were empty. Quiet filled the school. There was a sense of anticipation—

—and then the bell rang!

Doors burst open and students rushed into the halls. The school was buzzing with excitement!

In the gym, the stands were full of spectators, cheering and clapping. The school band was playing, the cheerleaders were dancing up a storm, banners were waving in the air. . . . It was time to decide who were the champions, once and for all!

In the locker room, Troy sat alone on a bench.

The rest of the team had run onto the court. He could hear the crowd being whipped into a frenzy.

All those hours of practice, all those drills, all that training . . . it all came down to this night.

His dad came into the room. "How're you feeling?"

"Nervous." Troy had to be honest.

"Me, too." His dad smiled. "Wish I could suit up and play alongside you today."

Troy grinned slightly. "Hey, you had your turn."

His father looked at him seriously. "Do you know what I want from you today?"

Troy nodded. His dad didn't have to tell him. "A championship."

His dad looked Troy straight in the eyes. "That'll happen or it won't," he said gently. "What *I* want is for you to have fun. I know about all the pressure, and probably too much of it has come from me. All I really want is to watch my son having the time of his life, playing a game we both love. Give me that, and I'll sleep with a smile tonight, no matter how the score comes out."

Troy looked at his father. A strange feeling of

relief spread through him. "Thanks, coa—" He corrected himself. "Dad."

His father smiled at him and walked away.

Blackboards had been set up on each side of the choir room—the first round of the Scholastic Decathlon was about to begin. The walls were lined with tables where contestants could conduct experiments. A few dozen chairs had been set out for judges and spectators.

As the clock ticked down, each team gathered for a final briefing.

In the theater, Kelsi played random tunes on the piano as a few spectators wandered into the large auditorium. Ryan and Sharpay did bizarre actor-prep exercises backstage: opening their mouths wide, uttering weird vocalizations, and falling back into each other's arms to demonstrate their absolute trust in each other.

In the choir room, the decathlon teams, all wearing lab coats, faced off for the opening bell.

Gabriella stood at a blackboard, poised to begin. The moderator signaled "go," and she and the star of the competing team began scribbling formulas as fast as they could.

In the theater, Ms. Darbus was making yet another speech. "Casting the leads of a show is both a challenge and a responsibility, a joy and a burden," she said. "I commend you, and all young artists who hold out for the moon, the sun, and the stars—"

The five kids sitting in the auditorium just stared at her. They didn't have a clue about what she meant.

Ms. Darbus sighed, and tried to end on a grand note. "So . . . shall we soar together?" She checked her clipboard, just for form's sake, and called out, "Ryan and Sharpay?"

The brother-and-sister team made a grand entrance as their recorded music started. From the very first note, it was clear that this was a two-person musical, with light cues and choreography and moves that would put most Broadway dancers to shame.

As they started singing the chorus, Sharpay and Ryan moved into all-out choreography, with kicks, spins, turns, and leaps.

Meanwhile, in the gym, the two teams who would be battling for the championship finally faced each other in center court. This was it—all the training, all the practice drills, all the pep talks led up to this . . . very . . . moment. . . .

The ref threw the ball for the opening tip-off, and the game began! From the very first seconds, the crowd was going crazy.

Even in the choir room, the Scholastic Decathlon team could hear the crowd noise. Everyone except Gabriella, that is. She was standing at the board, totally focused on what she had to do. As the timer ticked down, she and her opponent wrote formulas as quickly as possible.

Just one last number and she finished seconds ahead of her opponent and slammed the timer button, stopping the clock.

The moderator quickly checked her answer, then nodded. Points to the Wildcat Scholastic team! As everyone cheered Gabriella, whose face was flushed with victory, Taylor peeked at the clock. It was 3:35 P.M.

She quietly moved over to her laptop and punched in a code, murmuring to herself, "All right,

Wildcats, time for an orderly exit from the gym. . . ."

Immediately, the words "message transmitted" appeared on the screen. In the gym's utility room, a small wireless router had been patched into the electronic grid. Within seconds, the router started blinking . . . the mission had begun!

Suddenly, the electronic scoreboard blinked and random numbers began appearing where the score had been. The message board began flashing. The gym lights pulsed on and off.

The players stopped in midgame, baffled as to what was going on.

Principal Matsui didn't know what was happening either, but he did know school policy. He quickly took the mike and said, "Well, we seem to have a little electronic gremlin here. I'm sure we'll figure this out. In the meantime, per safety regulations, we all need to make an orderly exit from the gym—"

As the gym slowly emptied, Chad grinned a private grin. Phase one of the mission had been executed!

Back in the choir room, Taylor quickly hit another key on her laptop. A beaker of blue liquid was sitting on a nearby hot plate, waiting for the experiment section of the competition.

Taylor's click turned on the hot plate, which heated the liquid, which began to gurgle, which created pressure that popped off the top of the beaker—which released an awesomely bad smell in the room.

Taylor smiled in quiet satisfaction as she saw first the moderator, then the spectators, begin to react to the smell.

Within seconds, everyone had rushed out of the room.

Taylor nodded. Phase two had just been completed.

In the theater, Sharpay and Ryan were blissfully unaware of the other dramas that were taking place in the school. They ended their song with just as much energy as when they had started. They knew they had done phenomenally well, and they took extravagant bows.

"Do you see why we love the theater, people?" Ms. Darbus said, almost overcome with pride and joy in her star pupils. "Well done."

She made a quick check of her list and then asked, in an offhand tone, "Troy Bolton and Gabriella Montez?" She looked around. "Troy . . . Gabriella?"

But there was no sign of them.

Kelsi looked around nervously. "They'll be here!"

Ms. Darbus shook her head with little regret. "The theater, as I've often pointed out, waits for no one. I'm sorry."

Kelsi gave one more despairing glance at the door, but there was still no sign of her friends. She sank back onto the piano bench, crushed.

"Okay, we're done here," Ms. Darbus said briskly, drawing a line through Troy and Gabriella's names. "Congratulations to all. The cast will be posted."

Slowly, Kelsi picked up her music folder and left the stage, totally dejected.

Then Troy and Gabriella came dashing in from opposite sides of the theater.

"Ms. Darbus! We're here!" Troy yelled.

"I called your names," Ms. Darbus said sternly. "Twice."

"Please." Gabriella couldn't believe it. After all their work, all their planning . . .

The drama teacher was firm. "Rules are rules."

But as she turned to go, she saw that something different, unexpected, in fact, altogether astounding was happening! The theater was starting to fill with people: students and spectators from the basketball game and Scholastic Decathlon; all the members of the basketball team, led by Chad; all the members of the Scholastic Club, led by Taylor . . . they were all coming to watch the auditions!

Sharpay and Ryan watched the gathering crowd, confused. This wasn't part of their plan! Still, the theater is all about dealing with the unexpected, so Sharpay quickly said, "We'll be happy to do our number again for our fellow students, Ms. Darbus."

The teacher shook her head, still watching with amazement as the theater filled to capacity. "I don't know what's going on here. But, in any event, it's far too late, and we don't have a pianist."

Ryan and Sharpay smiled, relieved. Ryan

looked at Troy and shrugged. "Oh, well, that's showbiz," he said happily.

Desperate, Troy said, "We'll sing without music."

Then they heard a voice—previously a timid voice, now a surprisingly bold one—call out, "Oh, no, you won't!" Kelsi charged onto the stage. "Pianist here, Ms. Darbus!"

Sharpay gave her a warning glance. "You really don't want to do that."

Kelsi set her jaw. She had had enough of taking orders from egotistical drama queens. "Oh, yes, I really do!"

She opened the piano lid with a flourish, slapped down her music, and took a seat. "Ready onstage!"

Ms. Darbus's eyes widened with delight. "Now . . . *that's* showbiz!"

Troy and Gabriella picked up their microphones and turned to face the auditorium. It was packed with people, all waiting to hear them sing.

As Gabriella looked out at all those eager faces, she felt her face turn red. Then her knees got weak, and her stomach flipped over, and she thought she might faint.

Their first audition had been for Ms. Darbus, and they hadn't even known she was listening! Now she had to face this huge crowd.

Kelsi hit a piano key, waiting for Troy and Gabriella's nod that they were ready to begin. No one nodded. Gabriella was standing absolutely still, as if she were frozen.

Kelsi started to play, hoping that the music would help relax Gabriella and that she would start singing.

But Gabriella couldn't even open her mouth. Kelsi stopped playing and looked at Troy. What should I do?

He nodded to her to start again. And then he began to sing, directly to Gabriella.

*"We're soarin', flyin'*
*There's not a star in heaven that we can't reach*
*If we're tryin', yeah, we're breaking free"*

When it was Gabriella's turn, she covered her mike and said, "I can't do it, Troy. Not with all these people staring at me."

Troy glanced at the crowd. People were starting to look confused. They were murmuring to each other, "What's wrong? Is she all right?"

He turned back to Gabriella and whispered, "Look at me. Right at me. Like the first time we sang together, like kindergarten, remember?"

She did. And when she looked into Troy's eyes, he looked back the same way he did at the karaoke contest. The spark of magic flared up again, but brighter and stronger. Gabriella could feel herself relax. She could feel herself smile. . . .

Troy made a signal to Kelsi, and she started playing again. Troy sang, heartfelt:

*"You know the world can see us*
*In a way that's different*
*Than who we are"*

Gabriella smiled even wider and sang the next two lines:

*"Creating space between us*
*'Til we're separate hearts"*

Then they sang together, in perfect harmony:

*"But your faith*
*It gives me strength, strength to believe..."*

As they continued, their confidence—and their trust in each other—grew. They began to sing as though they were the only ones in the room.

Everyone in the auditorium was transfixed by the powerful, real emotion that Troy and Gabriella were expressing through the song.

Coach Bolton wandered into the auditorium, wondering impatiently when the electronic malfunction would be fixed and the game could resume. He looked at the stage—and he couldn't believe what he was seeing! His son was singing, in public, and—he was really, really good!

Throughout the theater, the music was casting its spell. The brainiac girls glanced at the basketball boys, and the two groups exchanged friendly smiles. The skater dudes nodded to the drama kids—hey, if this is musical theater, it's cool, man. All the different groups, usually so separate, were united as they watched a completely unlikely pair—Troy dressed in basketball warm-ups and Gabriella wearing a lab coat—sing to each other with genuine emotion.

As the song ended, Troy and Gabriella gazed into each other's eyes. For one long moment, there was total silence. Then Kelsi stood up and began applauding. So did Coach Bolton. Ms. Darbus called out "Bravo!" and "Brava!" over and over again. And then the entire crowd was on their feet, roaring their approval.

Even Ryan and Sharpay started applauding—then they caught themselves and quickly stopped.

Before the applause ended, Troy and Gabriella gave each other a quick hug and rushed off. After all, they had some unfinished business to attend to. . . .

# CHAPTER 9

It was the last few seconds of the championship game. The Wildcats were behind. The clock was ticking down. . . .

Then Troy suddenly flew across the court, weaving between opponents, heading for the goal. Just as he had practiced, he faked right, went left, threw the ball, and . . . NOTHING BUT NET! The buzzer sounded and it was a one-point Wildcat victory!

In the melee that followed, Coach Bolton found his son and gave him a huge hug.

Ms. Darbus fought her way through the crowd.

As she approached the coach, the old adversaries eyed each other for a moment . . . then they grinned and gave each other a high five.

As Gabriella got close to Troy, he called out, "What about your team?"

"We won, too," she said, excited and happy. They hugged each other in congratulations, just as Chad handed a basketball to Troy.

"Team voted you the game ball, Captain," he said. They high-fived each other, then he turned to Taylor. "So . . . you're going with me to the after-party, right?"

"Like on a date?" Taylor asked, shocked.

"Must be your lucky day." Chad grinned.

She laughed, and nodded. A week ago, she would have disagreed, but now . . . maybe Chad was right. Maybe it *was* her lucky day.

As Gabriella walked out of the gym, still beaming, Sharpay came up to her. "Well, congratulations," Sharpay said. "I guess I'm going to be the understudy in case you can't make one of the shows, so . . . break a leg."

Gabriella looked at her, startled.

Sharpay smiled—a real smile this time—and explained, "In theater, that means good luck."

And now Gabriella smiled a real smile, too.

As she moved on, Zeke saw his chance and moved in on Sharpay.

"Sorry you didn't get the lead, Sharpay," he said. "But you're still really, really good. I admire you so much."

"And why wouldn't you?" asked Sharpay, who hadn't changed into a completely different person, after all. "Now bye-bye."

He shyly held out a bag of cookies. "I baked these for you. . . ." She took them as if they were her due, and he walked away.

Troy found Kelsi in the crowd and handed her the basketball. "Composer, here's our game ball. You deserve it . . . playmaker."

Kelsi nearly fainted. *She* was being handed the game ball by *Troy Bolton*! She got dizzy just thinking about how much her life had changed in one short week. Dizzy and very, very happy. She broke into a huge grin and threw the ball in the air. . . .

And when it came down, East High School was a different place. It was a place where punk kids could talk to brainiacs, and jocks could hang out with drama kids. It was a place where everybody could follow the beat of their own drummer, and other people would cheer them on. In other words, it was a place where people could have fun . . . together.

After the huge celebration ended, people were still milling around, laughing, talking, and getting to know people they had never even noticed before.

That's when Sharpay came flying into the crowd, pushing people out of the way to get to Zeke.

"Your cookies are genius!" she yelled. "The best things I've ever tasted. Will you make some more for me, Zeke?"

Zeke grinned. *Of course* he would bake for her! In fact . . . he waggled his eyebrows and said slyly, "I might even make you a crème brûlée."

PRESENTING

Disney

# HIGH SCHOOL MUSICAL 2

EAST HIGH

The Junior Novel
Adapted by N. B. Grace

Based on *High School Musical 2*,
Written by Peter Barsocchini
Based on Characters Created by Peter Barsocchini

ROCK

STAR

The Future is a Big Place

## CHAPTER 1

The halls of East High School were eerily quiet. The auditorium was deserted. Not one sound echoed inside the cavernous cafeteria. In the gym, a lone janitor mopped the floor. No one was rushing up the stairs, no one was running down the hall. In fact, the only sound that could be heard was Ms. Darbus talking to her homeroom class. . . .

But no one, of course, was listening. Troy Bolton gazed at the wall clock as the minute hand jumped to 2:58 p.m. He glanced over at Gabriella Montez, who smiled back. Only two minutes until they were free!

Ms. Darbus seemed completely unaware of the fact that she didn't have everyone's rapt attention. "Learning is never seasonal, so do allow the shimmering light of summer to refresh and illuminate your fertile young minds," she said.

Sharpay Evans frowned at the ticking clock while her brother, Ryan Evans, gazed absently out the window at cloud formations. Chad Danforth struggled to keep his eyes open as he did a silent countdown to three p.m. in his head. Zeke Baylor seemed to be studying—but he had hidden *How to Bake the Perfect Muffin* inside his advanced algebra textbook and was actually reading about batter. Martha Cox's feet were dancing with impatience under her desk. Taylor McKessie sat with her hands folded on her desk, looking like the perfect student, even though she was as anxious as any of them for the bell to ring. And Jason Cross . . . Jason was actually taking notes on what Ms. Darbus was saying!

"Your future greets you with its magic mirror, reflecting each golden moment, each emboldened choice," Ms. Darbus went on. "So use these incipient summer days and weeks wisely and well. . . ."

Troy leaned over to whisper to Chad, "Ms. Darbus has snapped her cap."

Chad opened his eyes wide in surprise. "Dude," he said, "you're actually *listening*?"

Sharpay began tapping her fingers on her desk to the rhythm of the second hand. After a few seconds, she tapped even faster, willing the time to speed by, and turned to her brother. "Ryan, this semester of disappointment and humiliation now comes to a screeching halt, and the future begins," she whispered. "And that means—"

But Ryan wasn't listening. He was still staring out the window.

"Ryan!" she snapped.

"Is it me," he asked dreamily, "or do those clouds look like Jessica Simpson?"

As the students fidgeted in their seats, the sound of ticking seemed to get even louder, drowning out Ms. Darbus's voice. . . .

And the clock on the wall seemed to get bigger and bigger as everyone stared at it longingly. . . .

"Summers have passed fleetingly since I was your age," Ms. Darbus went on wistfully. "Yet I recall them with poignant clarity, so . . ."

Jason raised his hand.

"Yes, Jason?" Ms. Darbus said.

"What's your favorite summer memory, Ms. Darbus?" Jason asked.

The entire class groaned. What was Jason *thinking*?!

But Ms. Darbus was happy to answer him. "Ah, yes, the Ashland Shakespeare Festival of '88 leaps fondly to mind. In fact . . ."

*Claaannnggg!* Just in the nick of time, the bell rang . . . and the whole school erupted in cheers!

Classroom doors were flung open and students poured into the halls. It was time to say good-bye to school and hello to summer!

As Troy, Chad, Zeke, and Jason walked together toward their lockers, Troy said, "Dudes, when hoops camp is done, I've got to make bank. I keep hearing my parents talk about what college is going to cost."

"Yeah, my folks will match whatever I make this summer, but first I've got to get hired," Zeke said.

"Me, too," Chad agreed. "I'm saving for a car"—he nodded toward Taylor, who was standing across the hall—"so I can take that girl on a proper date." He expertly spun the basketball he was carrying. "Unfortunately, this is my only job skill."

His friends nodded ruefully. Getting a summer job wasn't going to be easy, especially since they were in high school. Still, nothing could dampen the excitement of the last day of school!

Talking and laughing, everyone headed for the front doors . . . but not without a few last good-bye rituals, like the signing of yearbooks.

Sharpay stood by her trademark pink locker and signed her name with a grand flourish. She occasionally flashed a smile at the student photographer who was snapping away with his camera, recording this celebrity moment for posterity.

Gabriella paused to watch what passed for a media frenzy in the halls of East High. Sharpay glanced at her and said, "I understand you've moved every summer for the past five years. I'd hate to think that today is"—she gave Gabriella a hopeful smile—"good-bye?"

Gabriella smiled back, but it was because she was so happy knowing that all the years of moving

135

from town to town had come to an end. "No worries. My mom promised I'm here until graduation next year," Gabriella answered cheerfully.

Sharpay's face fell. "Bless mom's little heart," she said insincerely.

Gabriella could feel the tension. She decided that this was the perfect moment to mend fences. Or at least try to keep them from completely falling apart.

"Sharpay, we got off to a rough start, but you came through," she said. "You helped me with the winter musical."

"I did?" Sharpay couldn't believe what she was hearing. When had she helped Gabriella? And how? And how could she make sure she never made such a mistake again?

Gabriella nodded. "Those breathing exercises . . ." She took a deep breath, held it for a moment, then let it out slowly, demonstrating what Sharpay had taught her.

"Delighted to assist a fellow Wildcat," Sharpay said in a tone that made clear she bitterly regretted offering *any* advice to Gabriella Montez. With effort, she added, "And, actually, I appreciated the opportunity to rest my voice for the spring musical."

"In which you were excellent," Gabriella said.

"So they say . . ." Sharpay said, gratified. Always ready to relive a triumph, she pulled a copy of the school newspaper from her locker. A huge photo of her filled most of the front page under a headline that read: SHARPAY SOARS.

"The second show on the third Friday wasn't everything it might have been," she said, "but the media is so easily impressed."

Then she tossed the newspaper back in her locker, where it landed on top of fifty other copies. Gabriella grinned and moved on to her own locker. At the other end of the hall, Troy, Chad, Zeke, and Jason were still talking about summer jobs, and now Taylor, Kelsi Nielsen, and Martha had joined in the conversation.

"Gabriella and I have had five job interviews, but we keep getting beat out by college kids," Taylor said.

"Same here," Martha sighed. "Guess I'm back in the baby-sitting business. Kelsi, what are you planning to do this summer?"

Kelsi looked up at Martha, who was a little taller. "Grow," she said wryly. She added the obvious "Write music." Then she glanced up at Taylor, who was a *lot* taller than her, shook her head and said again, "Grow."

Gabriella had almost finished cleaning out her locker when Troy snuck up behind her and wrapped his arms around her in a hug.

"Your summer activities consultant has arrived," he said in a teasing voice.

Startled, she looked around, and he grinned at her. "Me! After basketball camp, we'll see movies, download music, a little karaoke, and I'm definitely teaching you a twisted flip on the skateboard."

She laughed. "I have Red Cross training, so I can patch myself up afterward."

Sharpay was standing close enough to overhear their teasing, and she rolled her eyes.

"Hey, worse comes to worst, we just chill," Troy said. "As long as we spend summer together, it's all good."

Gabriella looked up at him. "Promise?"

He nodded as he pulled a necklace from his

pocket and handed it to her. "Here's my promise."

Gabriella's eyes widened with surprise as she saw the "T" hanging from the necklace. Across the hall, Taylor and Chad noticed this moment—and Chad, of course, had to make a joke. He pretended to offer her his basketball as a present, but she just gave him a withering look and turned back to see what would happen next.

For a moment, she thought Troy was actually going to kiss Gabriella. Until, that is, a couple of starry-eyed freshmen girls came squealing up to ask him to sign their yearbooks.

As he agreeably autographed their books, Sharpay turned to Ryan. ". . . going to movies, listening to music . . . and, golly, Troy, I have Red Cross training so you can teach me skateboarding," she said in a falsely sweet voice, mimicking what she had overheard. Then, in her own voice, she added, "What she really needs is new product for her wayward hair."

She saw Kelsi standing at her locker, watching the other Wildcats wistfully. "Cheer up, Kelsi, I have a summer job for you," Sharpay said. "Our rehearsal pianist is evidently moving."

"Or hiding," Kelsi said under her breath.

Sharpay's eyes narrowed. "Pardon?"

Ryan saw the warning signs of a real snit coming on, and he quickly jumped in. "Relax, Sharpay. It's summer. You get to do whatever you want. Everything changes."

At Ryan's words, Sharpay's head snapped around again, this time to give her brother that look of intense focus and concentration that always made him so nervous.

"What did I say?" he squeaked.

"You're so right, Ryan," she said. "After what I've been through this semester, I deserve a special summer."

Troy, Gabriella, Chad, Taylor, and the rest of their crew walked past, headed for the front doors. Sharpay watched them go, thinking hard.

"Ryan, who is the absolute primo boy at East High?" she asked.

Ryan rolled his eyes at the utter obviousness of the answer. "I think Troy Bolton has locked up that category, don't you?"

"And East High's primo girl?" she went on.

Ryan glanced warily at Gabriella.

"Just answer the question!" Sharpay snapped.

"Gosh, let me think," Ryan said as sarcastically as he dared. "You?"

Sharpay nodded with immense self-satisfaction. "Troy . . . Sharpay. Sharpay . . . Troy," she said musingly. "It just makes sense."

"Evidently not to Troy," Ryan pointed out.

But Sharpay wasn't listening to him. She was focused on the delicious plot that was beginning to form in her brain. "But it's summer, Ryan," she said, smiling. "Everything changes."

A few feet away, Kelsi took some sheet music from her locker and looked at Sharpay thoughtfully. What, she wondered, was the diva of East High up to now? Then she glanced down the hall and watched as the Wildcats burst out through the front doors into summer . . . and freedom!

# CHAPTER 2

Two weeks later, Troy, Jason, Zeke, and Chad were back from basketball camp—but that didn't mean they weren't still playing hoops every second they could. One evening, they piled into the Boltons' kitchen after their workout.

Troy's father, Coach Bolton, followed them, tossing them bottles of water. "What I saw out there just now looks very, very strong, guys," he said. "Camp really stepped up your game."

Chad yelled, "What team?"

They yelled back, "Wildcats!"

Just then, the phone rang. Troy answered it. As

he walked away from the guys, Chad said, "Uh-oh, girlfriend alert."

The other guys laughed, but Troy was already in the next room. The caller wasn't Gabriella. It was a man Troy had never met before—but who seemed to know an awful lot about him.

"This is Thomas Fulton over at Lava Springs," the man said. "I understand you've been looking for summer work?"

"Hey, Troy, does Gabriella still remember your name, or did she karaoke with someone new on vacation?" Zeke called out from the kitchen.

As the guys cracked up, Troy waved at them to be quiet. "That sounds fantastic, Mr. Fulton," he said. "But how did you get my name?"

"We've always had a student summer work program here at Lava Springs," he said smoothly. After a second, he added, "Go, Wildcats."

Okay, Troy thought, fair enough. But if it was a student summer work program, maybe there was a way he could make this sudden opportunity into something even more fun. . . .

"Here's the thing," he said. "I know this really great girl . . . I mean, *student* . . . straight A's, *quintuple* straight A's, and she's looking for a job, too, and it'd be so amazingly perfect if . . ."

He kept talking, pacing around the room as he tried to sell Mr. Fulton on his really great idea.

"Man, he's really working someone," Chad said.

"It can't be Gabriella," his father said. "When she calls, he just blushes." He looked at the guys, catching himself. "I never said that."

Finally, Troy was done. He hung up the phone looking pleased.

"What's up, dog?" Chad asked.

"Up?" Troy said with a grin. "What? Nothing."

He slapped the basketball out of Chad's hands and dribbled it around the kitchen, causing immediate chaos as everyone went after him.

"Hey, not in the house!" his dad yelled. "Troy's mother will be home in a minute, then we're all dead!"

They immediately calmed down.

"I'll tell you what, though," he added, "you stick together this summer, work on the game, and we're talking back-to-back championships next fall."

"Bet on it," Troy said with confidence.

His friends looked at him, curious. They could tell he had something up his sleeve. But what?

His dad took advantage of their momentary distraction to steal the ball. Instantly, the kitchen was again in an uproar, until the ball was snatched from midair and everyone turned to see . . .

. . . Troy's mom, holding the basketball and giving them her Mom Look. "Do you think we can all redirect this energy toward carrying in the groceries?" she asked calmly.

"Yes, Mrs. Bolton," everyone said—even Coach Bolton.

The Lava Springs Country Club was heaven on Earth—if you were a member. The clubhouse gleamed with brand-new paint. Tanned, happy people sprawled on chairs underneath the beach umbrellas that surrounded the swimming pool. On the patio, members enjoyed their lunch in the warm sunshine of a beautiful summer day.

It was the perfect day . . . until a convertible with license plates that read FABULUS rolled through the front gates. It purred up the driveway to the portico. A valet rushed forward to greet the driver . . . none other than Sharpay.

"Miss Evans, Mr. Evans—looking very sharp this summer," the valet said.

In the passenger seat, Ryan tipped his stylish hat in greeting.

"Thank you, David," Sharpay said, with just the right combination of reserve and warmth. "Can you find some shade for our car?"

Before the valet could answer, another voice said, "Even if we have to plant a tree, Miss Evans." Mr. Fulton stepped forward and added smoothly, "I trust that your vacation was satisfactory?"

Sharpay shrugged. "New York, for shopping and Broadway shows. Seven days, eight shows, eleven new pairs of shoes. However, it's good to be"—she looked around and sighed with satisfaction—"home."

She and Ryan got out of the car and walked with Mr. Fulton toward the clubhouse. Sharpay waved graciously to other club members and staff as she proceeded up the drive. A warm glow filled her heart as everyone responded to her greetings.

Now I know how the Queen of England feels when she returns to Buckingham Palace, she thought.

Then something caught her eye. "Is it possible to get more color in these gardens?" she asked. "I'm thinking yellows and blues."

Mr. Fulton nodded quickly. "Lovely." He snapped his fingers at a gardener and pointed to the flowerbed.

Sharpay smiled happily. It was so nice to be someplace where her slightest suggestion was treated as an order to be obeyed! If only the rest of the world operated like the Lava Springs Country Club, she thought.

As she and Ryan swept into the lobby, Sharpay caught sight of a display cabinet. There was her father's photo, with a nameplate that said Club Founder and President. There was her mother's photo, with a placard that read Director of Membership Committee.

Next to these sat gleaming trophies celebrating the Evans' triumphs in swimming, diving, tennis, golf, and ballroom dancing competitions that had been held at the country club.

Her gaze moved on to a poster advertising the club's next big social event: LAVA SPRINGS' ANNUAL MIDSUMMER NIGHT'S STAR DAZZLE TALENT SHOW! MAKE RESERVATIONS NOW!

Mr. Fulton pointed to a stack of programs lying on a reception table. "This year we embossed the flyers for the show."

"Inspired," Sharpay replied. She pulled out a marker and began autographing the flyers. "I plan to limit member talent auditions to thirty seconds each. Amateur performers are very . . ."

"Draining?" Mr. Fulton filled in helpfully. "Understood."

"And should I"—she paused and quickly included Ryan in her statement—"we be so fortunate as to win the Star Dazzle award again . . ."

"We're planning to widen the trophy case," Mr. Fulton said. "I have sketches in my office."

She beamed at him. Mr. Fulton was truly a treasure! "You are so efficient," she cooed.

This summer was shaping up to be the best one ever, she thought. So far, everything was going according to plan. She just had one other little matter to take care of. "The staffing matter

we discussed . . . ?" she whispered to Mr. Fulton.
"Handled, with discretion," he assured her.

"How . . . fabulous," she replied. Then she headed off to the locker room. Time to put the next phase of Operation Perfect Summer into motion.

# CHAPTER 3

A few minutes later, Sharpay emerged from the locker room wearing a gorgeous swimsuit, a cute cover-up, and a dramatic sun hat. She carried a brightly colored parasol and a shoulder bag stuffed with sunscreen, cell phone, makeup, flip-flops, and magazines.

She heard breathless greetings and turned to see three girls named Jackie, Lea, and Emma rushing over. They seemed thrilled to have spotted her.

A voice behind Sharpay said, "Your chaise in its usual spot, Miss Evans?" She turned to see a pool attendant hovering nearby.

"Wonderful, Javier," she said. "Emma and Jackie west of me, Lea east. And you'll be a prince to angle our chaises on the hour, as the sun moves."

He smiled. "Thanks to the kind words from your mother last season, I've been promoted, but I'll see to it that the new lifeguard is fully briefed on your requirements," he assured her.

Imagining herself a queen settling on her throne, Sharpay sat down. Her attendants—she caught herself—her *girlfriends* gathered around her.

"So what's the theme of the summer talent show, Sharpay?" Emma asked eagerly.

Sharpay paused dramatically, then said one simple word: "Redemption."

The girls exchanged confused glances, then Lea spoke for all of them. "Huh?"

Sharpay sighed. How could she explain what the last year had been like?

She settled for saying, "It was a very . . . trying . . . year, ladies." After a moment, she gathered her strength and went on. "My drama department was invaded by outsiders—singers coming out of the chemistry lab and locker room."

"It's over, Sharpay," Ryan said. He had emerged

from the locker room in time to overhear the last of her complaints. "It's summer, remember? We've got the pool and the entire club, and the whole summer to enjoy it."

"And the spa has been redone," Emma pointed out.

"There's an avocado facial and seaweed body scrub on the menu," Jackie added.

"It's all too perfect," Lea sighed happily.

"Oh, really?" Sharpay said. Nothing was ever *completely* perfect, after all. She frowned at her glass, then raised it in the air to get the attention of a waiter. "More ice, please."

If not completely perfect, life at the Lava Springs Country Club was definitely fabulous! And, the girls noticed, it had just gotten better. A cute guy was headed their way. They adjusted their sunglasses to get a better look. When they saw who it was, they exchanged surprised glances . . . everyone but Sharpay, that is.

The boy was none other than Troy Bolton, carrying a tray of drinks poolside. Sharpay smiled to herself . . . until she spotted Chad, Jason, and

Zeke being led toward the pool area by Mr. Fulton. Her smile disappeared. What was going on here?

And Troy didn't even notice her! Sharpay turned to follow his gaze—and saw Gabriella, looking beautiful in a lifeguard swimsuit, her hair flowing in the breeze!

Sharpay's mouth dropped open. She stood and took a couple of uncertain steps backward. Everywhere she looked, she saw nothing but Wildcats! It was all just . . . TOO . . . MUCH! Stunned, she took another step back and . . . *SPLASH!!!*

Sharpay floundered in the water, sputtering, hoping that this was just a terrible dream and that any minute now she would wake up—

An arm grabbed her around the neck and pulled her to the edge of the pool. Gasping, Sharpay turned to see Gabriella, who had dived into the water when she saw Sharpay struggling.

"What are you DOING HERE?!" Sharpay yelled.

"I'm the new lifeguard," Gabriella explained.

Troy looked confused. "Are *you* a member here?" he asked Sharpay.

Sharpay gasped. Was *she* a member? Was she a *member*? If Lava Springs Country Club had a royal family, she would be the princess! And right now, she was one very angry princess!

"**I** asked you to hire *Troy Bolton*, not the entire East High student body!" Sharpay screamed. She had Mr. Fulton pinned against the wall. Ryan was at her side, looking suitably outraged.

"Troy Bolton was insistent that Miss Montez have a job," Mr. Fulton said evenly. "She's Red Cross certified, you know."

"That's already been clearly pointed out to me!" Sharpay yelled. She wasn't sure she would ever get over the humiliation of being rescued by Gabriella.

"And Troy was most persuasive on behalf of his teammates," Mr. Fulton continued. "Something about working together, winning together."

Sharpay rolled her eyes. "Rah-rah, sis-boom-bah."

"You told me whatever it takes to hire Troy Bolton," the manager reminded her. "Well, this is what it took."

"Why didn't you warn me about the rest of them?" she wailed.

Mr. Fulton stiffened. "I did discuss the matter with the Lava Springs board, of course."

"The board . . ." Ryan looked from Mr. Fulton to his sister, his mouth dropping open as the truth slowly dawned. "You mean, our . . ."

"*Mother!*" Sharpay screamed.

It didn't take long to track Mrs. Evans down. She was in yoga class, doing the downward-dog position. Sharpay and Ryan took up the position themselves in order to talk to her.

"I thought it would be a lovely surprise, my darlings," Mrs. Evans said. "When Mr. Fulton informed me that Troy Bolton wanted more Wildcats here, I thought, how brilliant!"

"Brilliant?" Sharpay was outraged.

Her mother twisted into another position. Sharpay and Ryan did the same.

"Think about the future, kitten," Mrs. Evans said. "These are chums, not the fuddy-duddy Lava Springs members."

Sharpay reminded herself that it was bad manners to scream in the middle of a yoga class. "These are not my *chums*!" she said as loudly as she dared. "They'll steal my summer show!"

Her mother smiled serenely (yoga helped her a great deal when it came to dealing with Sharpay). "And what fresh talent you'll have for your Star Dazzle show!"

Sharpay forgot her vow to show good yoga-class manners. "Mother, did you *hear* what I just *said*?" she yelled. Frustrated, she turned to her brother. "Ryan, talk to Mother."

Ryan obediently twisted himself into a new position to smile at his mother. "Hi, Mom."

She beamed back at him. "Ducky! How's my dashing boy?" She nodded toward Sharpay. "Tell pumpkin if she worries too much, she'll get frown lines."

Sharpay stormed out of the class. If her mother wouldn't fix this situation, she'd deal with it herself!

Mr. Fulton was walking down the hall by the spa when he was suddenly pulled aside by a very angry Sharpay.

"I want them out!" she ordered.

Mr. Fulton sighed. "Your mother specifically said—"

"Don't mention that backstabbing yogini to me!" Sharpay said. She paused to think for a moment, then suggested, "If you can't fire them, make them want to quit."

He suppressed a groan. "Actually," he explained, "we do need the help."

Sharpay could tell she wasn't going to get her way this time . . . at least not completely. But she could still win the battle, even if she didn't win the war. "Well, if they think working here is going to be summer camp," she said in a steely voice, "they're in for a surprise."

Lava Springs' newest employees were standing around the kitchen, waiting to start their jobs. They looked at their geeky uniforms and tried to remember why they all wanted summer jobs. Oh, yeah . . . to put some money in the bank.

There was one particular Wildcat, however, who would have been happy to be there even if he didn't earn a paycheck.

"Chef Michael is going to teach me the art of Austrian flake pastry, and Sharpay's going to be where I work," Zeke said with excitement. "How much better can summer get?"

Chad rolled his eyes. "A real dream come true."

Zeke looked at him earnestly. "If you actually get to know her, she's—"

Chad shuddered. "Dude, be my guest."

"Hey, I had no idea about Sharpay," Troy said quickly. "Mr. Fulton just said there were Wildcats fans at Lava Springs and jobs were available. So let's go for it."

Suddenly, Mr. Fulton appeared from nowhere. He looked at them sternly. "Indeed, since your jobs will be fleeting if you continue to treat your employment as if it's recess."

Chad was insulted. "Recess? Sir, we're actually in high school."

Mr. Fulton sneered. "As evidenced by the little toy you seem to carry at all times?"

Puzzled, Chad glanced down at his hands. Oh. "It's a basketball, sir," he explained.

"Better known at Lava Springs as a non-approved recreation device," Mr. Fulton said as he took the basketball from Chad. He tossed uniforms at the Wildcats and snapped out their assignments. "Danforth and Bolton, waiters and, when needed, caddies. Jason, dishwasher. Miss McKessie, I'm told you're efficient . . ."

She beamed as he handed her a clipboard.

"You'll handle member activities. Keep me in sight at all times. Kelsi, piano at lunchtime and cocktail hour. That means mood music, not new music. Clear? Martha, chopping, cutting, and preparing plates. Please complete the summer with the equal number of digits that I assume you currently possess. Zeke, you'll assist Chef Michael in . . ."

As the chef pulled trays of fresh scones from the oven, Zeke said happily, "The promised land."

At that moment, Gabriella rushed into the kitchen. Mr. Fulton looked at his watch and raised one eyebrow.

"Um, Mr. Fulton, Your Excellency, sir, is it okay if we draw straws to see who has to wait on Sharpay?" Chad asked in an innocent voice.

"Henceforth, none of you will be *waiting* on *Sharpay*," Mr. Fulton said.

"Snap!" Chad grinned.

Mr. Fulton continued frostily, "You'll be *serving Miss Evans*."

Jason looked confused. "What's that?"

Mr. Fulton sighed. He'd spent so many summers training high school students, and he had so many more summers to go before he could retire . . . sometimes the thought made him weary.

"Always address our members as Mr., Mrs., or Miss. Let's practice," he suggested. He faced Jason and pretended to be waiting on him. "Miss Evans, would you care for lemonade?"

"Actually, I'm not Miss Evans," Jason said, feeling even more confused. "I'm Jason."

Taylor whispered to Gabriella. "This is going to be a long summer."

Mr. Fulton looked at Chad. "Mr. Danforth, summon your 'high school' expertise to demonstrate member protocol for us. Miss—"

Chad gritted his teeth and said, ". . . *Evans* . . . more lemonade . . . your royal blondness?"

Mr. Fulton decided that that would have to do. He faced his new summer employees and said, "Do clock in on time. Three infractions of

any kind and your employment is terminated."
He glanced at Gabriella and looked at his watch
again. "It would seem your break ended a minute
and a half ago, Miss Montez. Let's hope no members drowned in your absence."

He turned on his heel and exited the kitchen
as swiftly as possible.

"Okay . . . that man officially scares me,"
Martha said.

Chad nodded. "Suddenly I'm missing Ms.
Darbus," he admitted. "How sick is that?"

Troy decided it was time to get everyone
focused on the positive. "Guys, there's a hoop out
back, we get two free meals a day, and we only
wear geeky outfits when on duty. All for one, one
for all. Come on now, it's our summer."

They all brightened up.

"What team?" Chad yelled.

"Wildcats!" they all yelled back.

After a second, Jason asked the question he'd
been puzzling over for some time. "Does anyone
know what 'henceforth' means?"

# CHAPTER 4

Sharpay's fellow Wildcats did have a lot of work to do, and Mr. Fulton did not make it easy for them. They had to clean off dining tables as soon as a meal was finished. They had to cart dirty dishes to the kitchen. They had to push the drink cart around the club. They had to pick up used towels, arrange rolls in breadbaskets, and generally help out whenever they were needed, quickly and with a smile.

Mr. Fulton watched them closely, correcting them any time they made a mistake.

If Chad was too slow cleaning off the dining tables, Mr. Fulton told him to speed it up.

And when Gabriella missed a towel that had been left under a bush by the pool? Mr. Fulton told her to "secure the perimeter" by looking everywhere for lost flip-flops, used towels, and misplaced water bottles.

But when Mr. Fulton's back was turned, the Wildcats knew how to have fun.

If Troy had to take dirty glasses to the kitchen, he took a spin on the cart after he'd emptied it!

If Chad had to fill a dozen breadbaskets, he tossed the dinner rolls across the kitchen with a pair of tongs.

It was fun, but it was also tiring. At the end of another long day of work, Gabriella plodded into the employee room carrying an armload of used towels. She dumped them in a laundry bin, and slid her time card into the clock to punch out.

A hand reached over her shoulder holding another time card. She turned to see Troy looking down at her.

"Ever been on a golf course?" he asked.

"We're employees, Troy, not members," she reminded him. "And I don't play golf."

He raised his eyebrows. "Who said anything about playing golf?"

When they got out to the golf course, Gabriella saw that Troy had set up a picnic on the green just for the two of them.

She looked around nervously. "You sure it's okay to be out here?"

"Unless the jackrabbits turn us in," he said with a grin.

Gabriella laughed, feeling relaxed and happy for the first time all day.

But at that very moment, Sharpay and Ryan were standing on the roof of the country club. Sharpay whipped open a messenger bag that had slots for binoculars, walkie-talkies, and a digital camera. She frowned at Troy and Gabriella through the binoculars.

"I have no idea what anyone sees in her," she said through gritted teeth.

"Hard to figure," Ryan agreed. "Since coming to East High she's starred in the winter musical, won the Academic Decathlon, made friends with everyone on campus, and is dating the most popular boy in Albuquerque."

Sharpay tossed her head in disgust. "She's wearing last year's colors."

"And picnicking is a nonapproved golf-course activity," Ryan added.

But Sharpay wasn't listening. "I am an outstanding student—if you overlook math, science, social studies, and history. I'm a five-time Star Dazzle winner, have won three 'most innovative hairdo' badges from Girl Scouts, and am *massively* fashion forward. I've been at East High three years, and she's been there five minutes. Isn't it obvious that Troy Bolton deserves to be with me?" She handed him the binoculars.

"Somehow that doesn't seem like his immediate plan," Ryan observed.

"His plan's about to change," Sharpay snapped.

Out on the golf course, Gabriella was unaware that she and Troy were being watched. Instead, she was enjoying a perfect summer evening with Troy.

"So how's kitchen duty?" she asked.

"The team that washes dishes together, wins together," Troy said.

Gabriella nodded. "My mom said summer jobs look good on college applications."

"All part of that frightening concept called 'the future,'" Troy said glumly.

She gave him a searching look. "You sound a little worried."

"Hey, college costs a fortune," Troy said. "My parents are saving pennies. Unlike the people at this place."

"You're a cinch for a scholarship," she said.

He shrugged. "I can't rely on that. I'm only as good as whatever happens next season."

"Let's decide that the future doesn't start until September," Gabriella said. "I've never been in one place for an entire summer, Troy, and certainly never with—"

She stopped, suddenly feeling shy.

". . . a supremely gifted sandwich maker like me?" Troy said, rescuing her.

She smiled. "I want to remember this summer," she answered softly.

He jumped up, pulled her to her feet, and

began dancing with her in the warm light of the setting sun. Gabriella laughed as he dipped her, then pulled her up and twirled her around.

And, for the moment, the glow of the present made them forget all about the future.

That glow wouldn't last, of course. Not if Sharpay had anything to say about it

Mr. Hardy, one of the club's maintenance workers, had just put his feet up when his walkie-talkie squawked.

Sighing, he picked it up.

"Mr. Hardy, Sharpay Evans here," she said crisply. "When I was on the fourth fairway today, it seemed . . . bone dry. Could you give it a little extra splash?"

"Right away, Miss Evans," he said, happy that he wasn't being asked to do something major. He hit a few buttons and sat down again, ready to get back to some peace and quiet.

Troy and Gabriella's dance had just come to an end. They stood facing each other, leaning toward each other, on the verge of a kiss . . . when a dozen high-powered sprinklers came on, completely drenching them!

They laughed as they took off running. They were having as much fun as they did when they ran through lawn sprinklers as little kids.

Sharpay scowled as she saw that her prank had failed.

"That sort of looks like fun," Ryan said wistfully.

Sharpay lowered her binoculars. "Does it?" she said slowly as an idea formed in her mind.

She picked up her phone and punched in a number.

Seconds later, Mr. Fulton's phone rang. When he saw who was calling, he winced, but he did what he had to do. He answered it.

"**T**his is a private club, not a water park," Mr. Fulton lectured Troy and Gabriella, who were standing in front of him dripping wet. "We exist to serve our membership. Employees will do well to remember their place. Clear?"

Troy and Gabriella nodded meekly.

Mr. Fulton turned his laser eyes on Gabriella. "Late back from your break today, now frolicking on the golf course. We're not off to an auspicious start, Miss Montez."

Sharpay watched the lecture through her binoculars and said to Ryan, "Keep an eye on them tomorrow and keep me posted."

"Why are you smiling?" Ryan asked warily. "You're scaring me now."

Sharpay just smiled. "There's nothing to worry about, Ryan. This is *our* campus, remember?"

# CHAPTER 5

Early the next morning, Kelsi went to the country club's dining room and began to play a song she had composed.

In the employee room, Troy and Gabriella heard the music as they clocked in. They glanced at each other, and headed to the lounge. Ryan entered the room, but when he saw who was there, he hid behind a potted plant. As he listened to Kelsi play, he began to look concerned. This song was excellent.

"Whoa, sounding good, Wildcat!" Gabriella said.

Kelsi immediately stopped playing and covered the music. "Actually, I have to get ready for the ladies' bridge luncheon. I won't exactly be rocking out." She glanced over at her friends and added excitedly, "But we'll all really have fun in the club's talent show, because employees do a number and I've got ideas for everyone. . . . You guys sing lead, and Zeke and Chad and everyone can do backup and maybe dance, too, and . . ."

Behind the potted palm, Ryan whispered into his walkie-talkie, "Goldenthroat, this is Hatboy. We may have trouble."

**S**harpay and her mother were in the spa, their faces slathered with avocado. As Sharpay listened to her brother's walkie-talkie, she raised one eyebrow. Very interesting . . .

**B**ack in the dining room, Troy held up his hands to stop Kelsi. "Club talent show? Whoa, whoa!" he said. "Big time-out on that one. My singing career began and ended with the East High Winter Musical. I'm only here to make a check and sneak into the pool after work."

Kelsi's face fell. "Oh."

Ryan smiled. Sharpay will be relieved to hear this, he thought as he left the dining room.

Troy looked at Gabriella. She'd back him up on this, right?

Gabriella asked Kelsi, "What was that piece you were playing a minute ago?"

"Oh . . . nothing." Kelsi shrugged. "It's really just . . . nothing."

Gabriella picked up the sheet music and turned it over. At the top of the page, were the words "Troy and Gabriella's Song." Eyebrows raised, she said, "What's this about?"

Kelsi looked sheepish. "I was thinking if you guys did a show next year at school . . . you know . . . I wanted to be ready."

Once Ryan was outside by the pool, he called his sister again on his walkie-talkie. "You want the bad news or the good news?" he asked.

"Just spill it, Ryan!" Sharpay snapped as a beautician put cucumber slices on her eyes. She took a sip from her smoothie. "I'm busy!"

"I heard Kelsi working on an amazing new song,

and she didn't write it for us," he whispered. "But the good news is that Troy announced that he doesn't want anything to do with our Star Dazzle show."

Gabriella glanced over at Troy as she said to Kelsi, "Well, can we at least hear the song you're working on? It does have our name on it. . . ." Kelsi hesitated, so Gabriella reached over and played the first few notes. That was enough. Kelsi sat down and began to play.

After a few moments, Kelsi was playing with such total concentration that she didn't even notice when the other Wildcats poked their heads in from the kitchen to listen.

When she finished playing, however, she did hear something: wild applause as her friends burst into the dining room.

"Wow, I love that song," Gabriella said.

"I've got the talent show sign-up sheet right here," Taylor said. "The kitchen staff said it's really fun. How about it?"

Everyone nodded in agreement, but they looked at Troy. What would he say?

"Well, I guess we could croak something out if we had to," he said. "But it's got to be all of us."

Kelsi signed Taylor's sheet as the other Wildcats all gave each other high fives.

Sharpay took a sip of her smoothie. "I've been thinking, Ryan, it might actually be a wonderful idea if Troy participates in our show."

Ryan frowned. "But if he sings with Gabriella, our talent show is going to be . . ."

"Oh, I'm not certain Gabriella is ideally suited to help Troy realize his full potential here at Lava Springs," she said airily. She turned to her mother. "Mommy, what time is Daddy going to be here?"

"We tee off at noon," her mother replied. "Join us?"

"Wonderful," Sharpay said. She pulled a cucumber off her face and ate it with a loud snap.

Later that day, the Wildcats were busy in the kitchen. Martha was chopping vegetables, Zeke was baking, Jason was washing dishes, and Troy and Chad were putting food on a serving cart.

Only Kelsi had some time off, so she was thumbing through music at one of the prep tables.

Suddenly Mr. Fulton appeared carrying two white coveralls. He tossed them to Troy and Chad, barking, "Danforth, Bolton, you're caddying today. Forty bucks a bag. You've been requested."

"By who?" Troy asked.

"Who cares?" Chad said, delighted. "For forty bucks I'd caddy for Godzilla."

"That's the spirit," Mr. Fulton said.

Troy and Chad walked to the first tee and saw Sharpay and Ryan waiting.

"Hi, boys!" Sharpay said happily. "So, Troy, I thought it was time for you to meet my parents."

Troy shuddered. "Meeting the parents" sounded like something a boyfriend would do. Still, he smiled politely and shook hands with Sharpay's mother.

He looked around. "So . . . where's your dad?"

As if on cue, a stretch limo rolled into the parking lot. A man wearing expensive golf clothes stepped out and strode over to them.

"Where's the first tee and what's the course

record?" he called out. He saw the boys gaping at him and chuckled. "Just kidding . . . I built the course myself and hold the record. But who's counting?"

He gave Sharpay a big hug and slapped Ryan on the back. Then he turned to Troy and Chad. "So . . . quite a season you boys had."

"Troy played for the golf team, too, Daddy," Sharpay said sweetly.

Her father looked impressed. "Versatile." He asked Chad, "What about you, son?"

"Track and field," Chad said.

Mrs. Evans laughed. "Might come in handy today, with the way I play golf. Fair warning."

Sharpay beamed as she handed Troy her father's golf bag. This meeting couldn't be going any better if she had scripted it herself—which, in a way, she had.

Her mother teed off, sending her ball off into the rocks that edged the course. Then her father hit his first shot. The golf ball sailed into the air. The game had started.

Sharpay got into her cart and rolled across the green. She had her very own golf cart, of course. It was pink and included a DVD player, an ice chest, and a smoothie maker.

Soon Mr. Evans was asking Troy's advice before every shot. At the ninth hole, Troy sized up the lay of the land, then said, "One forty-three to the pin, downhill lie, elevated green. I'd go with the seven iron, sir."

Mr. Evans swung his golf club. He watched as the ball sailed through the air and landed right next to the flag! "Nice call, son," he said.

Sharpay applauded. Troy smiled modestly and then looked around for Chad, who was knee-deep in brambles, looking for a ball that Ryan had sliced into the woods. As a branch nearly hit him in the face, he resolved that he would never complain about washing dishes again.

At that moment, Sharpay hit her golf ball. Chad and Troy both had to dive to the ground to avoid being hit in the head.

"Why don't you take up knitting, Sharpay?" Chad suggested. "That way you can only injure yourself."

As the day went on, Troy was surprised to find that he was actually having fun. It was sunny, and he enjoyed helping Mr. Evans play a good game. If Sharpay and her ridiculous pink cart hadn't been there, he wouldn't have had a care in the world.

As he and Mr. Evans walked past the clubhouse on their way to the next hole, he looked over the fence surrounding the pool. He saw Gabriella sitting on her lifeguard stand and said, "Dinner tonight? Then sneak a swim?"

She nodded happily, but as she watched him rejoin the Evans family, her smile dimmed. Sharpay handed Troy a cold drink. Even from a distance, Gabriella could tell she was flirting with him—and Troy was smiling!

He has to be nice to her, Gabriella thought, trying to be fair. That's his job.

But still, she felt her heart sink a little as she watched them walk across the grass.

After the golf party had played several more holes, Sharpay suggested, "Daddy, why not let Troy try a shot?"

Mr. Evans was so impressed with Troy's golf tips that he agreed without hesitation.

Troy smacked the ball onto the green, and the Evanses all applauded. In that moment, Troy felt a change. He wasn't a caddy working for the Evans family anymore. Now he was another golfer playing with them.

Sharpay floored her golf cart to pick up Troy.

Chad had to dive for the ground, this time to avoid being run over. "I'm saving up for a car, saving up for a car," he murmured to himself.

Troy hit another great shot, and the Evans family oohed and aahed.

"Tiger Woods would have been proud to hit that shot!" Mrs. Evans exclaimed.

"Absolutely," Sharpay said, adding casually, "and what a shame that a potential all-star for the University of Albuquerque Redhawks is busing dishes in the kitchen."

Her father took the bait. "They've got Troy working in the kitchen?" he asked, shocked.

Troy hit another shot. The white ball flew into the sky in a long, graceful arc.

Mr. Evans watched the perfect shot and said, "I've seen Troy play basketball. And I'm sure the Redhawks will be interested in his future."

Chad shot a suspicious look at Sharpay. What was she up to? he thought.

"That's inspired, Daddy," she said warmly. "Troy is very concerned about college."

Her father smiled at her, pleased. She smiled back, even more pleased. Everything was going according to plan.

# CHAPTER 6

Later, Chad sat in the kitchen, his sore feet immersed in an ice-filled bucket.

"Next time I see country club princess, I'm gonna launch her and her pink cart straight into the pool," Chad promised.

Mr. Fulton came into the kitchen and frowned at him. "Mr. Danforth, this is a kitchen, not a nail salon. You and Jason suit up for lunch duty in the dining room." He handed Troy a blue blazer and tie. "Bolton, you've got five minutes to change and come with me."

Surprised, Troy followed Mr. Fulton out the door.

"What's with the tie and coat?" Taylor asked.

"Maybe it's a country club version of detention," Jason suggested.

The others looked worried. They didn't know why Troy was being asked to dress so formally—but they knew it probably meant trouble.

Mr. Fulton led Troy, now nicely turned out in coat and tie, into the dining room where Sharpay and her father were seated with some other club members. Chad and Jason began pouring iced tea for the table as Mr. Evans said, "Let's talk about your future, Troy."

Troy looked at him, confused. "My . . . future?"

"Daddy's on the board of directors at the University of Albuquerque," Sharpay explained.

"Yep, we've got plenty to talk about," Mr. Evans said. "But first"—he turned to Jason and Chad—"bring on the food!"

Yes, the Wildcats were happy to have jobs.

Yes, they all needed to save money for college.

And yes, they all should have been working at that very minute.

But they were concerned about Troy. As Chad and Jason pushed food carts out to Troy's table, the others peered from the kitchen door into the dining room.

"What are they doing to him?" Martha asked in a hushed voice.

Zeke shrugged. "Who knows, but that pancetta-wrapped foie gras with seared bay scallops looks amazing," he offered.

"Look, Troy's trying to figure out which fork to use," Kelsi said.

As if she had heard this, Sharpay speared a melon ball with her own fork and fed it to Troy.

"Problem solved," Taylor said dryly.

While Chad and Jason served the food, they heard a member say to Troy, "I saw your championship game. Wow, that shot at the buzzer—"

Troy caught Chad's eye. Quickly, he said, "My teammates stole the ball, or I wouldn't even have had the chance to—"

"Oh, Troy, you're much too modest," Sharpay broke in. "You were voted MVP for the entire season." She leaned over and retied his tie, saying,

"This shirt positively screams for a Windsor knot."

"A what?" Troy couldn't believe it! She was dressing him in front of all these people! He had never felt so mortified in his life!

Gabriella joined her friends at the doorway.

"What's she doing?" Gabriella asked.

"Fixing his tie," Kelsi guessed.

"Or strangling him," Taylor added grimly.

"What are they all talking about?" Gabriella wondered just as Chad passed by with yet another serving tray.

"How Troy single-handedly saved the planet," he said sarcastically.

Just then they heard a foot tapping behind them, and they turned to see . . . Mr. Fulton! Quickly, they scattered back to their jobs. Fortunately, Kelsi had to return to the piano and could watch what happened next.

"We've got a heck of a basketball program at U of A," Mr. Evans was saying. "And an excellent scholarship program."

That got Troy's attention. "Scholarship?"

"Between the bunch of us here, we pull a little weight at the school," Mr. Evans continued. "And it's never too soon to be thinking about your future, son."

Troy suddenly remembered that he'd promised to meet Gabriella. "Oh, man, I'm supposed to clock out. Mr. Fulton will—"

"Nonsense!" Mr. Evans cried. "You haven't had dessert, and we haven't talked golf."

"Basketball and golf are just the beginning with Troy, Daddy," Sharpay volunteered. "Have you heard him sing?"

*What?!* Troy quickly said, "Singing? No, no—"

One of the men at the table chuckled. "A singing point guard? Now this I gotta hear."

"Maybe at our Star Dazzle Talent Show," Sharpay said. "Oh, give them a sample, Troy." She turned to cue Kelsi.

"My voice is a little hoarse today," Troy croaked as convincingly as he could. "But thank you so much for the golf and food. It's all been . . . great."

"So . . . you will sing some other time, though, right?" Sharpay asked.

"Promise," he finally said, feeling trapped.

"Perfect!" Sharpay exclaimed. "Dessert?" She signaled for Chad and Jason to bring the dessert cart. Éclair or tiramisu? Or maybe as a celebration, she'd have both!

By the time Troy had finished his dinner, all of his friends were gone for the night.

He headed outside to the pool, where he found Gabriella cleaning up.

"Sorry I'm late!" he called across the pool. "Just give me a few more minutes!"

She nodded and called back, "Nice tie. Shoes don't match, though."

He rolled his eyes at the teasing and ran back inside to clock out. Just as he was putting his time card into the machine, Mr. Fulton appeared.

"Don't clock out, Bolton," he said.

"But I'm done for the day, sir," Troy replied.

"Evidently not," the manager said. "Your presence is required in the ballroom."

Troy thought of Gabriella, waiting for him—but then he looked at Mr. Fulton's face, which had a don't-even-think-about-arguing expression on it.

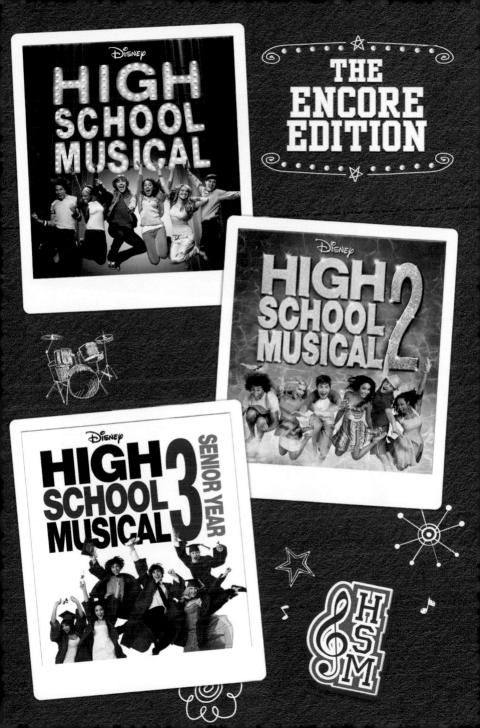

When Troy and Gabriella sing together for the first time, they forget how nervous they are about performing in front of a crowd.

Gabriella is shocked to see Troy in the hallway of her new school, East High, on her first day.

Gabriella meets Taylor, who invites her to join the Scholastic Decathlon team.

Troy's best friend, Chad, doesn't understand why Troy wants to audition for the musical. As the basketball championships near, he wants to make sure Troy keeps his head in the game.

**HIGH SCHOOL MUSICAL**

Sharpay and Ryan are a little too proud of their audition for the school musical, but the Drama Club superstars aren't quite good enough.

Troy and Gabriella sing together, and their harmonies meld so perfectly they win the lead roles in the high school musical production.

East High students celebrate summer—Wildcat-style!

Troy and his friends are thrilled to get summer jobs at the country club, even though Mr. Fulton is a stern boss.

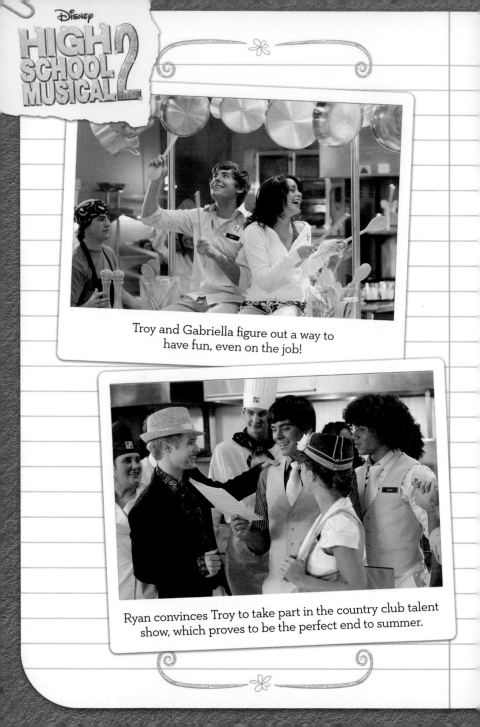

Troy and Gabriella figure out a way to
have fun, even on the job!

Ryan convinces Troy to take part in the country club talent
show, which proves to be the perfect end to summer.

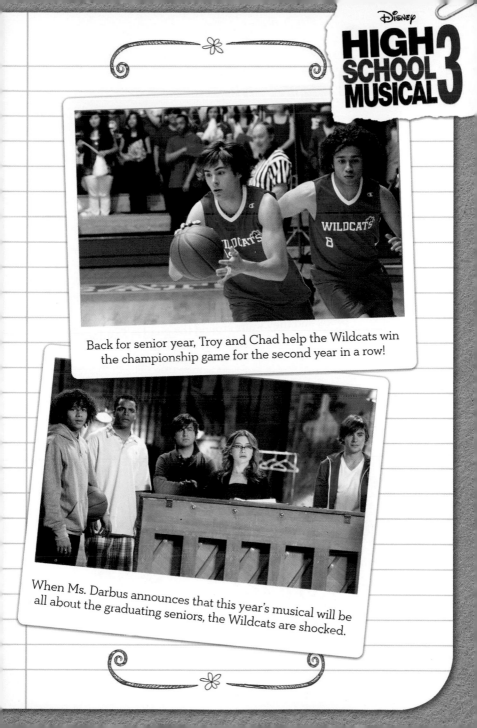

Back for senior year, Troy and Chad help the Wildcats win the championship game for the second year in a row!

When Ms. Darbus announces that this year's musical will be all about the graduating seniors, the Wildcats are shocked.

Troy surprises Gabriella the night of the East High prom, and they waltz around the quad at Stanford. It's a night to remember.

Wildcats FOREVER!

He sighed and followed the manager to the ball-room, where there was a sign that read: CLOSED REHEARSAL/NO ADMITTANCE.

Holding a flashlight, Mr. Fulton led Troy to a chair in the darkened room.

"What the heck . . . ?" Troy started to say.

But Mr. Fulton was gone.

Suddenly, the darkness was broken by a brilliant spotlight, which was shining on—of course—Sharpay. She was standing center stage wearing a Hawaiian princess costume, complete with a pineapple on her head. She was joined by Ryan, Jackie, Lea, and Emma, doing a Hawaiian tiki number that involved a chorus of "humu humu" and "waka waka."

Troy stared at the stage, his mouth hanging open. Sharpay was singing and dancing her heart out, and Ryan was reaching for the rafters with every note.

Troy was afraid to move. He felt as if he'd been trapped inside a megamusical machine.

Out by the pool, Taylor was giving her girl Gabriella some no-nonsense advice. "Honey, ten minutes is being late . . . but an hour is approaching a felony."

"We just talked about having dinner," Gabriella said. "No big deal."

"Just because Troy is a nice guy doesn't mean he's immune to boy disease," Taylor said.

Gabriella raised one eyebrow. "Boy disease?"

Taylor gave her a meaningful look. "Forgetting things he shouldn't forget."

Gabriella laughed. "So now you're a boy expert?"

"My older sister has ten rules about boy behavior, and nine involve boys forgetting things they shouldn't forget," Taylor said. She added pointedly, "Like dinner dates."

"It wasn't an official date type of thing," Gabriella said, trying to be fair.

Taylor shook her head. "Rule three: all dates are official, whether the boy knows it or not." She paused, then said, "Chad and I are going for pizza with Zeke and Jason. I think Martha and Kelsi are going to meet us. So let's go—"

Gabriella hesitated.

"I'll meet you there," she finally said. "Troy will probably want to come, too."

Taylor sighed. She certainly hoped Troy's case of boy disease didn't get any worse!

# CHAPTER 7

When the Hawaiian tiki number was finally, mercifully, over, Troy applauded politely.

Sharpay jumped down off the stage, beaming at him. "So?" she asked. "You love it?"

Troy hesitated, eyeballing the pineapple on her head. "Look, do you ever just . . . sing? Without lights, sets, and all the backup people?"

Sharpay gave him a puzzled look. "It would be much harder to get applause that way."

"I'm not talking about applause . . . or volcanoes," Troy said. "I'm talking about hanging with friends. Doing nothing. Singing for fun."

Sharpay considered this. "Wait a minute, not doing anything . . . that might work." She paused. "A dark stage," she said dramatically. "A single spotlight. We break out of darkness into the circle of light. . . ."

"We?" Troy asked uneasily.

But Sharpay didn't seem to hear him. "No set, no frills. Just you and me," she went on. "Simple, dramatic. That's a wonderful idea, Troy! We could do it in our club talent show."

When Ryan overheard that, a tiny frown wrinkled his forehead. What was Sharpay talking about? *He* was singing with her in the club talent show. . . .

Troy looked horrified. "I'm here to work," he said. "Saving money for my . . . future. Being onstage is really your thing, not mine."

She smiled at him sweetly. "It could be . . . *our* thing," Sharpay said coyly.

"What?! Whoa. I've already got an 'our thing' with Gabriella, which I'm very late for at the moment."

"But the show could be so . . ." Her voice trailed off, but she was still gazing at him.

Troy had to get out of there—now! Trying to distract Sharpay, he blurted out, "Hey, those are *really* nice shoes you're wearing."

Sharpay glanced down. "You like them? I bought them in New York. I have them in nine colors."

And when she looked up, Troy was gone.

Gabriella had finally finished picking up all the wet towels when she heard someone behind her yell, "CANNONBALL!"

Troy came running across the deck and jumped into the pool, fully dressed.

"Whoa, you're crazy, Wildcat!" She laughed.

"And *so* late," he admitted. "But I have food. A candle for a poolside picnic. And Zeke made desserts." He grinned. "But first, I dare you . . ."

She grinned back. "I've got to go put my suit on," she began.

"What happened to Miss Fun Kindergarten?" Troy said.

"CANNONBALL!" she yelled as she leaped into the water.

They both started laughing hysterically and splashing each other.

"Hey, you have no idea what I just saw," Troy said. "I'll never be able to look at a pineapple again."

"Huh?"

He laughed. "Never mind. You know, right now with you, it's finally feeling like summer."

"Yeah." Gabriella smiled. "It is."

They moved a little closer to each other in the moonlight, romance fairly shimmering in the air, but just as they were about to kiss—

"Well, well," Mr. Fulton said. "The water bugs are back."

Troy and Gabriella, startled, whirled around as Mr. Fulton turned on a flashlight and leveled its beam at them. They climbed out of the pool.

Troy gulped. "It was my idea, Mr. Fulton, she didn't . . ."

The manager shook his head sternly. "You have a reason to be here after-hours, Mr. Bolton. Miss Montez, however, does not." He frowned at Gabriella. "I overlooked the tardiness yesterday.

But then came the golf-course jaunt, and now this. Two days, two strikes. Don't get a third."

He walked back into the clubhouse. Just inside the door, Sharpay smiled—she'd seen the whole thing.

Later that evening, Troy took his basketball out to the driveway to shoot some hoops with his dad. After a few minutes, he said to his father, "Sharpay's dad let me play a few holes today. Then he introduced me to some U of A alumni in the dining room."

His dad quit guarding him for a second. "What alumni?"

Troy took advantage of the opportunity to sink a basket. "Mr. Sherwood, Mr. Langdon. They're members at Lava Springs."

"I played ball with those guys," his dad said, pleased. "I'll give them a call. This is great news."

"Really?"

His dad nodded. "Shaking hands with influential alumni doesn't hurt."

"But they were talking about scholarships right in front of Jason and Chad, who were like . . . serving food to me," Troy said.

"And getting paid for it," his dad pointed out. "It's called a job. You were invited, nothing wrong with that."

Troy shrugged. "It felt weird."

"I love that you've got the team working together at the club," his dad said. "But senior year is coming up, Troy. You're not going to be a Wildcat forever. Team is about now, but everyone has their own future."

"I'm not sure what you mean." Troy was confused. Wasn't his dad always saying that to be a team leader he had to remember the team?

His dad sighed. "As life goes on, lots of dogs are chasing the same bones. But one dog gets there first. You've earned your opportunities, son. A scholarship is special because they don't give it to everyone."

Troy nodded. He wasn't happy about it, but he knew what his dad was saying was right. "I get it, Dad."

"Okay." Mr. Bolton nodded, then decided to lighten the mood. "So . . . how was the food?"

Troy smiled. "Insanely good," he admitted.

The next morning, Troy raced over to the pool before starting work, hoping to find Gabriella so he could apologize. She was in her lifeguard chair as Taylor led a water-aerobics class.

"Still haven't gotten all the water out of my ears," he said to Gabriella. "Didn't mean to get you in trouble."

"And vice versa," she said.

He smiled. "So maybe today we can—"

But he was interrupted by a muffled voice saying, "Oh, Troy?"

His smile faded as he turned to see Sharpay inside the clubhouse, knocking on the window to get his attention. She held up a handwritten sign that read: MR. FULTON'S OFFICE.

He turned back to Gabriella. "Anyway, what time is your lunch break?"

"Troy!" Sharpay cried, pointing insistently at her sign.

"One-thirty," Gabriella replied.

"The free cheeseburgers are on me," he said. "See you then?"

She nodded happily, and he went inside.

Taylor climbed out of the pool. "What's that girl up to?" she asked, as Sharpay followed Troy.

"Who knows?" Gabriella shrugged.

"Believe me," Taylor said darkly, "she does."

When Troy got to the kitchen to clock in, Kelsi was already there talking excitedly about the talent show. As Troy walked past them, the other Wildcats started saying something. It sounded like "Humu, humu!"

Troy stopped. He turned and stared at them.

They looked back innocently.

But as he walked on, they started in again. This time, they were saying, "Waka, waka!"

Shaking his head, he grabbed his waiter's jacket. As he was buttoning it, Mr. Fulton appeared.

Quickly, Troy said, "I'm sorry I'm a couple of minutes late, Mr. Fulton. And the pool thing last night, you can't blame Gabriella, she only—"

"I'm promoting you," Mr. Fulton interrupted.

Troy couldn't believe it. "You are?"

The other Wildcats were close enough to overhear this. They all exchanged surprised glances.

The manager cracked a tiny smile. "There's an opening as an assistant to the golf pros. Salaried job, no clocking in. You start immediately."

"But . . ." Troy was too stunned to finish.

"Five hundred dollars per week," the manager said.

"WHAT!!! Per week?! Oh, man, that's totally off the hook!" Troy managed to collect himself. "I mean . . . that sounds very . . . workable."

Mr. Fulton led Troy out of the kitchen, telling him his new duties as they walked. They ended up at a door with a sign that read: MEN'S LOCKER ROOM—MEMBERS ONLY. Inside, Troy got to see how the members lived. The locker room was nice. Really nice.

But he was too distracted to notice much. He asked Mr. Fulton, "I'll be teaching golf?"

"To kids," the manager said, rolling his eyes a bit. "Oh, the joy."

"I don't think I'm qualified," he protested.

Mr. Fulton sighed. "Show the little angels which end of the club to hold, tee up a ball,

198

then duck. There's more. The board is extending membership privileges to you for the summer. You have full use of club facilities. So be prudent, and"—he pointed to a locker with Troy's name on it—"congratulations."

"Whoa," Troy said.

Mr. Fulton snapped his fingers, and a locker-room attendant appeared holding a rack of fashionable new golf clothes for Troy.

Troy's mind was reeling. This was all happening so fast! Then he opened his locker and found a golf bag with new clubs. His name was emblazoned on the bag. He pulled out a five iron, took a couple of practice swings, and broke out into a huge grin.

"Save it for the first tee," Mr. Fulton said. "And to get there, this might come in handy."

He handed Troy a key. "That's for your golf cart. It's number fourteen. Same as your basketball uniform, I'm told. Questions?"

Troy looked from the clothes to the locker to the golf clubs to the key. "How did this happen?"

Mr. Fulton raised one eyebrow. "Evidently, Sharpay Evans feels you have untapped potential."

He lowered his voice to offer a little advice. "Young man, the future is a big place, and the Evans family has real clout. I suggest you take the ride."

Troy was still amazed, but he nodded slowly. Maybe Mr. Fulton was right . . .

# CHAPTER 8

Over at the pool, Gabriella was busy scrubbing tiles. She didn't mind working hard, but she couldn't help but feel a little resentful when Sharpay walked by looking amazing.

The other club girls and Ryan were lounging by the pool, working on their tans.

Sharpay struck a pose to show off her outfit. "Is the green piping too much?"

Just as she expected, Emma immediately said, "Green is so this year," and the other club girls nodded in agreement. Each of them wore a swimsuit in a different shade of green.

Sharpay spoke a little louder so that Gabriella would hear. "I'm taking a golf lesson from Troy Bolton, so I want to look just right."

Sharpay's friends sighed in unison. Troy Bolton! He was such a cutie!

As Sharpay left, she said to Gabriella, "The pool has never looked better! Brava!"

Gabriella just gritted her teeth and scrubbed harder. Ryan watched them from the other side of the pool. His sister had always acted this way, but, for some reason, today it was making him rather uncomfortable.

Over at the junior golf clinic, Troy ducked as a club whistled past his head. He tried to figure out how to get the kids to focus on the finer points of the game.

"Bolton, your eleven-thirty is here," one of the other golf pros called.

Troy looked up to see Sharpay waving at him. He looked back to the members of his junior golf clinic. All of a sudden, spending the morning with them didn't seem so bad.

★ ☆ ★

Ryan glanced over at Gabriella. She was still scrubbing tile. And it was so hot out. . . .

Before he knew it, he walked over to her. "If you ever decide to dump my sister into the pool, give me a warning so that I can be here."

Gabriella could hear the sympathy in his voice. She said, "Does she ever actually swim, or just *look* at the pool all summer?"

Ryan laughed. "Sharpay doesn't allow her hair near water without shampoo, conditioner, and blow dryer within reach." He hesitated, then added shyly, "Look . . . um . . . I just want to say that I think it's cool that you're here. Last year's lifeguard was fat and had a hairy back."

Oops. That hadn't come out quite right.

But Gabriella just said, in a teasing voice, "I guess that's a compliment."

"Oh, absolutely," he said, fumbling to say something that sounded cool. "I mean, entirely."

She decided to help him out. "It was fun watching you dance in the spring show, Ryan. Especially when Sharpay wasn't dancing in front of you. You were amazing."

"*Really*?" Ryan's heart skipped a beat.

"Like, big-time." She smiled. "I'm looking forward to seeing you in the club talent show."

There was a brief silence. "Okay, well . . . thanks again," he said. "I mean, not for what you just said about my dancing, but for just being here. By the pool. On a nice day and everything. I guess they pay you to do that, right?" He stopped. He had *totally* lost where he was going with this! "I guess I'll swim now. I'm not that good a swimmer, but . . . lifeguard on duty . . ."

As he walked to the edge of the pool, Gabriella said, "Ryan? You want to put on a swimsuit."

He looked down. Oh. Right. He was still wearing his street clothes.

"Point taken," he said sheepishly.

*T*hwack! Sharpay hit a golf ball with a wild swing as Troy looked on. The ball went flying to the right.

*Thwack!* This ball veered wildly to the left.

*Thwack!* Her next ball headed toward a group of club members, who ducked.

Taylor rounded up the junior golfers for another activity, but she kept a close eye on Sharpay and Troy. She knew that girl was up to something!

Another ball whizzed off in the wrong direction. Troy didn't think he had ever seen a worse golfer.

"By the end of summer you'll have me playing like a pro," Sharpay said cheerfully.

He ducked away from one of her wild swings and muttered, "If I live that long."

She smiled and swung again. "I'm so excited about the Star Dazzle Talent Show. We'll find something great to do."

Troy sighed. "I already told you that's not for me."

She ignored him and went on. "Here's the best news: all the Redhawk coaches and the whole scholarship committee will be there."

Even from a distance, Taylor could see Troy reacting to something Sharpay had said. Reacting with interest and even . . . pleasure. She shook her head in disapproval.

"Really?" Troy said.

"Of course," she said casually, "Daddy and Mommy are on the university booster board. We'll lock up your scholarship with a high C, right from center stage." She added, "We're all in this together, right?"

Troy shook his head. He had to hold firm. Besides, he'd promised Gabriella and the other guys that he would sing with them. "Your family is being very nice, Sharpay. But singing with you isn't part of my job."

"I know," she said sweetly. "It's just something you promised to do. Remember?" She paused to let him take that in, then said, "You look fabulous in your new clothes, by the way."

He knew she was working him, but it always felt good to get a compliment. He said, "You like the shoes? They're Italian."

Taylor overheard this comment, and wished she hadn't. She rolled her eyes in despair.

Troy decided it was time to go back to the lesson. He moved forward to show Sharpay the proper— and, he hoped, safer—way to swing her club. He put his arms around her, helping her to adjust her grip.

Just then, Gabriella came out of the clubhouse carrying two boxed lunches. Her smile vanished when she saw Troy with his arms around Sharpay.

Taylor met up with Gabriella just as Chad came outside. Taylor nodded toward Sharpay. "That girl has more moves than an octopus in a wrestling match."

"I don't see him running away," Chad said.

"Troy can handle himself," Gabriella said. Now Troy was laughing at something Sharpay said as he moved closer to help her with her swing again. The two of them looked very, very cozy. Gabriella's heart sank a bit.

"Think so?" Taylor said. "He's asking her for her opinion on his new 'Italian' golf shoes."

Gabriella's heart sank a bit more. "He didn't ask me."

"So wake up, sister," Taylor said. "Sharpay is basically offering him a college education just to sing with her in the talent show."

"He'll never do that," Chad protested.

Taylor shook her head. Everywhere she looked, she saw the same thing: denial. "You got eyes?" she said to Chad. "Use 'em."

As Troy helped Sharpay set up another shot, one of the golf pros walked over. "Fulton wants you in the lobby, Troy." Troy nodded and hopped in his golf cart, heading off for the clubhouse.

Once he was gone, Sharpay put a ball on the tee, swung—and smacked it straight down the fairway! She smiled in satisfaction. Of course, she had been taking lessons forever—but Sharpay was nothing if not a great actress.

When Troy hurried into the lobby, he was surprised to see Mr. Fulton and Sharpay's dad—along with three star players from the University of Albuquerque basketball team!

"Troy Bolton, this is—" Mr. Evans began.

"I've seen them all play at U of A," Troy interrupted, impressed.

"Come scrimmage up at our gym tonight," one of the players said.

Troy gulped and glanced over at Mr. Evans. "Play . . . with you guys?"

The player smiled as if he knew how Troy was feeling. "You're in, bro."

"Wow," Troy said. "That's awesome!"

"Excellent," Mr. Evans said. "Now let's all get some awesome lunch."

Troy's head was still spinning when Sharpay scurried up to him and held a tie in front of his face. "I knew it!" she cried. "Coral blue. It's perfect for your skin tones. And mine, too. We're majorly skin-tone compatible, Troy."

"I have no idea what that means," he said, dazed.

"You don't need to," Sharpay said. "I'm here for you." And pretty soon, she thought, you won't know how you got by without me!

**A** short time later, Troy was hanging with the Redhawks on the terrace. He couldn't believe it, but they actually wanted his advice—about golf! As they sat down to eat, a cheeseburger was placed in front of him. He was so caught up in the moment that he didn't even look around as he said, "Actually, I think I asked for Swiss on the burger."

Behind him, Chad couldn't believe what he

just heard—and he had now officially had enough! He started to pull off his jacket, ready to rumble right there, when someone grabbed his collar and pulled him back.

"Table three needs more iced tea," Mr. Fulton said into his ear.

Chad went to the other table, then burst into the kitchen, where Gabriella and Taylor were eating lunch.

"You were right," he said to Taylor. "There's a guy out there who looks just like Troy, but I don't know who he really is."

Later that day, Ryan and Kelsi were sitting at the piano when Sharpay swept into the room and headed straight to them.

Ryan brightened when he saw her. "Hey, Kelsi's got great ideas to spark up the show," he said enthusiastically. "She—"

"I'm thrilled," Sharpay said tersely. She turned to Kelsi and snapped, "That duet you were playing the other morning for Troy and Gabriella, I'm told it's very good. I need it."

Kelsi tried to sound brave. "Actually, that's not available."

Sharpay gave Kelsi a dangerous stare. "Repeat?"

Kelsi felt her firm resolve waver a bit, but she said, "It's something I wrote *for* Troy and Gabriella. In case they—"

"You're an employee here, not a fairy godmother," Sharpay said. "Transpose the key. Troy and I will be doing it in the talent show. And brighten up the tempo a little bit. We'll need to keep people awake after the other member acts."

She headed for the dining room but Ryan jumped up and grabbed her.

"What about 'Humu Humu'?" he asked.

Sharpay sighed impatiently. "Change in plans."

"What am I supposed to do with my tiki warrior outfit?" Ryan protested.

"Save it for Halloween, go to a luau, sell it on eBay, I don't know," Sharpay snapped. "But in the meantime, keep an eye on those Wildcats. If they're planning on being in the talent show— which I doubt, once they hear about Troy and me—I don't want any surprises." She paused, then added graciously, "And I'll find a song for you somewhere in the show. Or the next show."

"Really? Don't strain yourself, slick," her brother muttered. Then he stalked off.

Sharpay shook her head. "Entertainers are so . . . temperamental."

# CHAPTER 9

Five, four, three, two, one . . . Yes! It was five o'clock and the workday was finally over! Everybody else was getting changed for the staff softball game that evening, so Gabriella wandered outside the kitchen and found Troy in the back, shooting hoops.

"Look at you," Gabriella said, taking in the new U of A warm-up jacket he was wearing. "Go, team."

"It's a gift from the guys," Troy said, half-sheepish, half-proud.

"The 'guys'?" Gabriella said. "Oh, you mean all those tall people?"

She stole the ball from him and took a shot.

"Right, the Redhawks," Troy said, going for the loose ball. "I've got to go in a minute, but I'll be back in an hour or so. Then can we go to a movie? Promise?"

Gabriella gave him a long, thoughtful look. "'Promise' is a very big word, Troy."

He hesitated. He knew what she was getting at, but he'd been so busy. "I know. . . ."

"And we've got the staff softball game tonight," she reminded him. "Remember, you 'promised' that you'd play?"

"Right . . . softball . . . tonight," he said, trying to cover. "I'll absolutely meet you there."

But he couldn't fool Gabriella. "You forgot, didn't you?"

"No, I just got the days mixed up," he lied. "I'm really sorry about missing lunch today, too. It's been wild. I can't believe how things are working out here."

"Italian golf shoes, new clothes, golf carts," she

214

said coolly. "That's crazy stuff. Hard to keep track of it all, I bet."

"That's just for my job," he said defensively.

"Right . . . the future," she nodded. "That's all I used to worry about, too. Never took my nose out of a book. Then I came to East High, lifted my head up, and liked what I saw." She paused, then added, "It's easy to lose that, I think."

Just then, Chad, Zeke, and Jason burst out of the kitchen, ready to play ball.

"Let's see if the Tiger Woods of Toon Town still has a jump shot," Chad said.

That's all it took to get a fast game going among the four of them. Before they had even warmed up, however, they were interrupted by a car pulling up and honking for Troy. The three Redhawk players were there to pick him up.

"Hey, tell them to come over here and mix it up," Zeke said. "We'll give 'em some game."

Troy said awkwardly, "I don't think that's how they roll."

Chad looked at him in disbelief. "That's not how they 'roll'? You think you're on ESPN or something?"

Troy blushed. "We're going to be working out with their coaching staff, I meant."

"Gee, you think maybe you can get us a video?" Chad asked sarcastically.

As Chad stared at Troy, Zeke said, "Yesterday you said we had a two-on-two for after work. Before the softball game."

Chad shook his head. "Zeke, that was so yesterday. You know, when we were all a team."

Troy didn't like leaving everyone mad at him, but the Redhawks were waiting. As he headed toward the car, Chad called out, "Yo, Bolton . . . that's my ball!"

Troy tossed him the basketball and got in the car. As the car pulled away, Jason said, "Will you guys be mad if I ask him to get me one of those cool Redhawk jackets?"

Chad and Zeke groaned and shoved Jason who looked, as always, confused.

"What?" he asked.

# CHAPTER 10

O n the eighth hole of the golf course, the Wildcats and the rest of the club staff were in the middle of a softball game. A boom box played in the background as teammates cheered each other on. Life didn't get much better than this!

Back in the parking lot, Gabriella and Taylor fired up a golf cart to head over to the game. They spotted Ryan on the way to his car and called out, "Hey, Wildcat, no rehearsal tonight?"

Ryan stopped in his tracks, surprised and a little wary of this friendly greeting. "My sister is working up something new for the talent show," he admitted. "Without me."

"So, you know about the staff softball game tonight?" Gabriella asked.

Ryan felt a faint stirring of hope. Was she actually asking him? No, it wasn't possible. "I'm not staff," he said.

"And I'm not much of a softball player," Gabriella said cheerfully. "So let's go!"

Ryan wasn't sure why she had asked but he didn't care. He hopped in the cart with the girls, and they rode off into the warm summer night.

It was the end of an inning. A few Wildcats wandered over to the cart where Gabriella and Ryan were watching the game.

Chad frowned at Ryan. "Did Fulton send you out here to spy on us?"

"Nah," Ryan answered. "My sister did."

"What?" Chad asked.

Everyone looked at him, stunned. Ryan was a little stunned himself—he had always been completely loyal to Sharpay, no matter what. And he was beginning to realize that he'd finally had enough of her. He laughed out loud at how free he suddenly felt. He added, "She thinks you guys might upstage her talent show."

"No worries," Zeke said. "We talked about doing the show, but it looks like Troy has bailed on us. So, whatever."

"What do you mean 'whatever'?" Gabriella asked. "It's our summer, remember. I thought we decided doing the show would be fun?"

Martha raised her hand. "I think so!"

"Who are we kidding?" Chad said. "We don't know what we're doing."

Gabriella pointed at Ryan. "He does."

Everyone looked at Ryan, surprised. He looked back, equally astonished.

"If we had a real director putting it together, we could be great," Gabriella went on. She turned to Ryan. "Have the employees ever won the Star Dazzle award?"

"Hey now," Ryan said, a shock of fear and excitement running through him at the very thought that Sharpay *might not win.*

"I know what you can do, Ryan," Gabriella said. "So why not do it for us?"

Chad had heard enough. They were athletes, after all, not artists! "Look," he said to Ryan, "if you want to hang, grab a mitt and let's play ball. But we're not dancers, so let's get on with the game."

Ryan heard the dismissive tone in Chad's voice and felt a flare of anger. "You don't think dancing takes some game?" he asked.

He stared right in Chad's eyes.

Chad stared right back.

It was a throwdown!

Even as the other Wildcats tried to explain that they didn't dance, and couldn't possibly learn in time for the talent show, Ryan had them doing some baseball moves: throwing, catching, sliding, running bases, and swinging the bat. Then he turned each action into a high-energy dance step, and pretty soon the Wildcats were moving and grooving all over the baseball diamond. The improvised dance ended up with Chad sliding into home plate.

Chad got up, dusted himself off, and eyed Ryan with new respect. "I'm not saying I'm going to dance in the show, but *if* I did . . . what would we do?"

Everyone turned to look at Ryan. He looked back, feeling both anxious and something else. He noticed they were smiling at him, and he realized what he'd been feeling—a sense of belonging.

Troy was in the middle of the hardest scrimmage of his life. He was breathing hard as he did his best to outrun, outmaneuver, and outjump guys who were bigger, stronger, older. . . .

It was work, but it was also really fun.

Troy's dad sat in the stands, watching the practice closely. Sharpay's dad was next to him, keeping his eye on this prospective new recruit that his daughter liked so much. And the University of Albuquerque's Coach Reynolds was under the hoop, noting every move, every step, every block that his players made.

Coach Reynolds blew his whistle for a water break, then walked over to Coach Bolton and Mr. Evans. "I like what I'm seeing," he said.

"Troy gives one hundred and ten, twenty-four seven," his dad said. "That you can count on."

Coach Reynolds nodded thoughtfully. "Have him work on that step-back move. He's got to be able to shoot over the tall dudes."

"Troy hasn't even started growing," Coach Bolton said quickly. "I grew four inches in college. But we'll be working on the step-back, believe me."

Meanwhile Troy wasn't thinking about growing four inches, or working on a step-back move. He was on the sidelines, using his cell phone.

On the golf course, the softball game had started back up. Gabriella was in the thick of the action, so when her cell phone rang, she didn't hear it. When Troy's picture came up on the screen, she didn't see it. The phone rang and rang, but was never answered. . . .

Later that night, Troy finally drove his dad's truck out to the baseball diamond. The field lights were on, so he hopped out and jogged to the diamond—but it was deserted. All his friends were gone. Troy stood for a long moment at home plate—alone.

Gabriella wrinkled her nose as the smell of chlorine wafted through the morning air. She began getting the pool ready for the day.

Then she looked up to see Ryan strolling toward her. He was wearing a pair of wildly patterned surf Jams in the Wildcat colors.

"Yo," she said, blinking at the crazy design. "Whoa, Wildcat!"

"Too much?" Ryan asked.

She laughed. "Only in daylight. East High colors, very impressive!"

He relaxed and grinned. "Be true to your school, right?"

"Absolutely," she nodded. Speaking of the Wildcats, that reminded her . . . "And everyone's psyched about the show."

He shrugged, but he looked pleased. "I know they all think I'm Sharpay's poodle, but—"

She held up a hand to stop him before he could become too apologetic. "If they thought that before, they're not thinking it today," she said firmly. He looked unconvinced, so she decided to bolster his confidence. "How do you do that swing-step thing you did last night?"

She awkwardly tried to re-create the move.

Ryan shook his head and said, "More like this . . ."

He demonstrated the move, then he grabbed her hand and spun her around—right into Troy!

Troy, who had decided to stop by to say hello to Gabriella, jumped back in surprise.

"Hey," she said, trying not to look as flustered as she felt.

"Hey," he answered, trying not to raise his eyebrows at the sight of Ryan and Gabriella dancing together.

"Hey," said Ryan, trying to think of something else to say that would ease this awkward moment.

Nope. Nothing came to mind.

Finally, Troy said to Gabriella, "I tried to call. I got . . . hung up at the gym."

"My dad said you did real well with the college guys," Ryan offered.

"They're awesome!" Troy exclaimed. His enthu-siasm took over. "Playing with those guys is like another world. . . ."

"Go, Redhawks," Gabriella said flatly.

Troy's excitement died down. "Really, I tried to call both you and Chad, but . . ."

Gabriella pointed to Ryan. "We were busy get-ting schooled."

Ryan grinned at the compliment, but Troy looked confused—and felt a little left out.

Just then, Mr. Fulton appeared in that sudden, spooky way of his and tapped on his watch. "Pool not quite ready, Miss Montez? We open in five minutes." He gestured toward Troy. "Mr. Bolton, I think you're due on the golf course."

Troy headed for the clubhouse as Gabriella, sighing, went back to work.

The guys were in the employee locker room put-ting on their work clothes when Troy came in.

"Hey, how'd it go with the Redhawks?" Zeke called out.

"They're very . . . tall," Troy said. That seemed

to sum up his first scrimmage with college guys as much as anything.

"We got Vince from maintenance to play," Zeke said. He didn't want Troy to forget that he'd let them down. Again. "So it worked out."

"Maybe we'll play later today," Troy said.

But his friends had already heard too many empty promises.

"Check with Vince," Chad said coolly.

Troy was starting to get annoyed. They were acting like this was all his fault. Did they want him to turn down a golden opportunity to scrimmage with the Redhawks just so he could play softball? "Mr. Evans set up the workout, not me," he pointed out.

Chad wasn't going to let him off that easily. "You ask to include us? Or maybe you ran out of room on your 'to-do' list."

Now Troy was more than annoyed. He was mad. "I didn't go looking for the Redhawks; they came to me. I didn't sign up for this golf job; Fulton offered it. But I said yes. My choice. Because it's fun, and it's stuff I should be doing for my future. I show up to work, same as you."

Chad had to roll his eyes at that last one. "Oh, please, if you get a speck of dirt on your pants, someone dry cleans you. You order off the menu, we eat what's left."

Troy said hotly, "You'd be doing the same thing, if . . ." He stopped, just a little bit too late.

"If we were as good as you?" Chad filled in the rest.

"I didn't say that." But Troy knew he almost had.

"We voted you captain of the Wildcats not because you've got a good jump shot, but because you're the guy who's supposed to know what's up," Chad said. He added bitterly, "That was before the summer, though, wasn't it?"

"You think you've got me all figured out?" Troy said. "I don't think so."

Just then, Mr. Fulton came in, took a look around, and said, "Gentlemen, you're not being paid to play Dr. Phil. Recess is over. Get busy." He turned to Troy. "Bolton, Mr. Evans wants you to meet him over at Indian Hills Country Club to golf with a couple of his business partners. He left you the keys to his Ferrari."

He handed Troy the keys, and Troy left without bothering to say good-bye.

The other Wildcats looked at each other.

"Ferrari?" Jason repeated. "All right, I admit it. Troy's a superior being."

"Yeah," Chad muttered. "Just ask him."

# CHAPTER 11

For the next few days, all the Wildcats were busy, busy, busy.

Troy played more golf games with Mr. Evans and the other Redhawks boosters. They listened to his golf tips, slapped him on the back when he made a great shot, and treated him to fabulous dinners at the country club. This was definitely the good life, and Troy couldn't help loving it.

Ryan had a blast rehearsing the Wildcats dance number for the talent show—and they were surprised to find that they were having an awesome time working with him. Of course, they couldn't let Sharpay know what they were doing! Fortunately, she was busy rehearsing with Troy and Kelsi, organizing the show, and trying not to wince when she saw some of the other talent that was going to take the stage.

Zeke kept creating new and better gourmet treats in the kitchen. And when Mr. Fulton had a bite, he was quietly stunned by how good the food was. When they weren't working, the Wildcats still had fun—but Gabriella sometimes found herself looking for Troy, and feeling sad when he wasn't there.

Troy kept playing in the Redhawks' scrimmages. He was loving every minute of his introduction to college ball—but he did feel let down when he went to the kitchen to find his friends, only to discover that it was empty. And even though it was great to be out on the golf course, it didn't seem quite as much fun now that he never saw his friends.

But that was the way the summer was turning out. Troy and the Wildcats now lived in two separate worlds.

★ ☆ ★

A few days before the talent show, a crew arrived to put up a party tent. Troy arrived at the country club and walked over to take a look.

Crew members were rigging lighting, putting up sets, checking sound equipment. Troy's jaw dropped in amazement. This wasn't some little pup tent—it was a showcase!

Sharpay was looking at the seating chart with her mother. When she saw Troy, she waved him over and pointed to a table that was highlighted in red marker. "Daddy will make certain the entire scholarship committee is right here," she said. "Perfect view."

"And I've invited your parents as our guests," her mother said. "It'll be a grand evening."

Troy looked around at the huge tent, the massive stage, the lighting, the decorations, the whole luxurious, over-the-top atmosphere. Then he looked at Sharpay, who was dressed as if she belonged in the pages of a fashion magazine. He had to admit it: Sharpay and the life she lived had a lot going for them.

Sharpay led him onto the stage. As Kelsi began to play, Martha and Taylor poked their heads into the tent.

And suddenly, like it or not, Troy was singing a duet with Sharpay.

It was the music that had been written for him and Gabriella, but Sharpay's changes had made it something completely different. When he sang the duet with Gabriella, the music had seemed beautiful and emotional. Now, it was a Broadway-style extravaganza.

He did his best to sing the way he knew Sharpay wanted him to, but his heart wasn't in it. In fact, he felt as if he were trapped in a nightmare—and had no way out!

"Good thing there isn't a panel of judges," Martha said, watching him struggle.

Taylor nodded. "My sister's boy rule number seven: when boys mess up . . . they *really* go all out."

Finally, the song ended. Sharpay took Troy's hands and looked deep into his eyes. "You know, Troy, I've always known you were special. And it's pretty obvious that I'm special. I think we were meant to sing together, don't you? I'm so excited for your future, it's just all worked out like a dream come true."

But when he looked back at her, he saw her wearing a lavish wedding gown and holding a bouquet!

He could hardly speak. He was terrified.

"Troy?" Sharpay said.

"I need some air," he said quickly.

As he headed for the door, she called after him, "Don't be long, we need to run it again!"

Once Troy was outside, he took off. He didn't stop until he got to the place where he always felt happy and in control: the basketball court. He grabbed a basketball and started taking shots. After a few minutes, he stopped in frustration. He couldn't help but notice that most of his shots were clunkers.

Then he heard something. Music and laughter . . . coming from the exercise room. . . .

Sharpay was getting annoyed. Troy had run out the door as if he were escaping something, and now, at least three—she checked her watch, no, five—minutes had gone by, and he still wasn't back.

She marched out of the clubhouse to look for

him. As she walked past the pool, she saw shadows coming from the members' gym. She walked over to peer through the windows . . . and gasped as she saw the Wildcats rehearsing a dance number directed by her very own brother!

Scowling, Sharpay watched as these . . . these *nobodies* danced and sang and laughed. What Sharpay didn't see was that Troy was looking through the windows on the other side of the gym, thinking wistfully that his friends seemed to be having a great time. And that Gabriella looked beautiful. . . .

When the rehearsal was over, the Wildcats left the gym after a few last hugs and jokes. Ryan stayed behind to collect his rehearsal notes and the CDs and boombox he'd been using. He was just about to head for home himself when the door swung open and Sharpay stormed in.

"I said keep an eye on them, not turn them into the Pussycat Dolls!" she yelled.

He grinned. "Pretty cool, huh?"

Sharpay was so astonished, she could barely breathe. "What are you doing to my show?! Do you want me to lose the Star Dazzle award to a bunch of . . . dishwashers?"

Ryan lifted his chin defiantly. "Your show? I'm part of a different show now, remember?"

"When did you become . . . one of them?" she demanded.

"Hey, that's a compliment," he said. "But you have a good show, Sis."

"Oh, I plan to," Sharpay said to herself as he walked away.

# CHAPTER 12

Sharpay went straight to Mr. Fulton's office. "The Midsummer Night's Star Dazzle Talent Show means something to me, and to my family," she said. "Those Wildcats will turn it into one great big farce."

"Your brother is one of 'those Wildcats,' I'm told," he countered.

"Don't mention that traitor to me," she snapped.

"Employee involvement in the Star Dazzle show is tradition," he pointed out.

"Traditions change," she said, dismissively. "My parents have important guests coming. We'll need every employee on duty that night, and not on the stage."

Mr. Fulton hesitated. "You might want to think this one out."

"All right." Sharpay paused a nanosecond, then said, "Done. Now do it." She stormed out of the office, feeling slightly happier.

Mr. Fulton caught sight of himself in a mirror. "What are *you* looking at?" he said guiltily.

The next day, Mr. Fulton handed Taylor a stack of memos. "Distribute these in the staff area," he ordered, "but not until end of shift."

"Of course," she said. Then she read the memo. "What?! Wait! But . . ."

"No discussion, Miss McKessie," Mr. Fulton said. "This is a business. I'm sorry to be the one to tell you, but welcome to the world of adults who have jobs they wish to keep because they have mortgages they wish to pay . . . tuition bills, car payments, etc. So sometimes there are tasks, however unpleasant, required by employers in order for the aforementioned and all-important paycheck to arrive in your all-too-empty pocket!"

After a moment, Taylor said quietly, "May I get you a cup of tea, Mr. Fulton?"

"That would be lovely, thank you," he replied.

A short time later, a glum group of Wildcats were gathered in the kitchen.

"How are we supposed to do a show if we've got a full shift?" Martha asked.

"I think that's the point," Taylor said.

Gabriella entered the kitchen, and Taylor handed her a memo. "Nothing we can do. Fulton's orders," Taylor explained.

Chad snorted at that. "No way this is Fulton's idea, unless Fulton suddenly has blond hair and wears designer dresses."

Gabriella finished the memo, her eyes wide. But she wasn't just upset. She was angry.

Sharpay was packing her pool bag when Gabriella stormed over to her.

"Forget about the rest of us, how about the fact that your brother has worked incredibly hard on this show?" she said heatedly.

"Oh, boo-hoo." Sharpay shrugged. "He'll be in

the show. He's a member. And don't lecture me about Ryan, given the way you've been interfering with Troy's future."

Gabriella's mouth fell open. "What?"

"You've gotten him written up by Mr. Fulton for sneaking onto the golf course, swimming after hours . . ." Sharpay pointed out. "I had to step in just to save Troy's job. He is worried about his future, worried about college, and all I've tried to do is help."

"What's that got to do with messing with our show?" Gabriella asked.

Sharpay glared at her. "You recruited Ryan because you're jealous of what I've done for Troy."

"I'm not talking about Troy," Gabriella said, frustrated. "I'm talking about my friends, your brother, my summer."

Sharpay rolled her eyes. "Oh, please. You don't like the fact that I won."

"What's the prize? Troy? The Star Dazzle award? You have to go through all this to get either one?" Gabriella yelled. "No thanks, Sharpay. You're very good at a game I don't even want to be a part of. Your club, your world, and you're welcome to it. But just step away from the mirror long enough to see who gets hurt when you win."

I could respond to that, Sharpay thought, I simply choose not to. So, instead, she grabbed her bag and stalked away.

Troy entered the kitchen, hoping to find everybody still there. The room was empty except for Taylor, who was looking pretty bummed.

She hadn't been too friendly to Troy lately, so he thought he'd say something light to brighten her mood. "If I have to teach one more junior clinic, I'm going to need a suit of armor."

"Might not be a bad idea," she said.

She handed him a memo. He read it, then said, "Oh, man . . . this is messed up."

"Like you didn't see it coming?" she asked.

He shot her a look. "What's that mean?"

"It's pretty obvious that big stage is just for you and your new best friend, Sharpay," she replied.

Troy's mind went immediately to the one person he did *not* want to think that. "Does Gabriella think that's what I want?"

Taylor shook her head. "Boyfriend rule number ten: wake up and smell the coffee, dude!"

"Where is she?" Troy asked.

Taylor shrugged. "Don't know. She told me this is her last day at Lava Springs."

*"What?"* Troy cried. He had to talk to her, he had to change her mind. He rushed outside and bounded down the steps, just catching Gabriella as she was packing her shoulder bag.

"You can't leave," he said breathlessly.

"Us working together sounded good, Troy, but things change. Right?" she said sadly.

"So give me a chance to make them change again," he said.

She gave him a serious look. "The talent show is a huge deal for Sharpay. It's a big deal for your future, too. That's cool."

He was shaking his head. She totally had the wrong idea, he had to set her straight. . . . "The golf, the singing, I'm just trying to work out this scholarship thing."

"Except when I talk to you, I don't know who I'm talking to anymore."

Troy felt a chill. "It's me."

A spark of anger appeared in Gabriella's eyes. "Blowing off your friends, missing dates? If that's you, it's good to know."

"I just need to get through this show," he explained.

"All I know is if you act like someone you're not, then pretty soon that's who you become," she said.

Troy stopped. He was afraid, deep down inside, that she was right.

"When I said I haven't had a summer in one place for five years, that was the truth," she said. "I want it to be special, and this isn't the place for that to happen."

A little desperately, he said, "I meant what I said about movies, skateboarding, and being together."

"I'm sure you did," she said coolly. "At the time."

"I'm just trying to catch up with it all."

She nodded. "Me, too. Because summer's happening, and I'm going to go find it. But I'll see you in September."

**F**ighting back tears, she walked into the kitchen and began to empty her locker. She remembered how much she'd looked forward to a summer with all her new friends . . . and Troy. She knew that it wouldn't do any good to stay in this job, hoping that the summer would end up the way she planned. No, she had to go her own way and make sure she had a summer she'd never forget.

When she left the kitchen, Troy was waiting. She knew that he had his own path to follow as well, and she couldn't really blame him.

A car honked. She looked at Troy. "Gotta go."

As she walked to the parking lot, three people watched her leave, all feeling different emotions.

Troy felt confused and sad. He had messed everything up and he wasn't sure how to fix it.

Taylor felt angry with Troy and upset to see Gabriella go.

And Sharpay felt nothing but a deep satisfaction. Everything, she thought, is working out *perfectly*.

That night, Troy was sitting alone in his room when there was a knock on the door. His dad came in, holding a plate of ribs.

"Usually you're taking these right off the grill," he said. He could see that his son was upset about something.

Troy shrugged. "Maybe I've been eating too much at the club."

His dad tried again. "Thought you'd be inviting the guys over for these ribs. I bought a couple extra slabs."

Troy hesitated, then said, "Do you think I seem real . . . different to you, dad?"

"You dress a lot better than usual," Mr. Bolton said, trying to lighten the mood a bit. He looked at Troy more seriously. "What's up?"

"Gabriella is quitting because she thinks I'm going overboard working the scholarship thing. I'm just doing the show with Sharpay because she's hooked me up with the boosters and all that. I don't really care about the golf, and playing with the Redhawks is cool but not if my guys don't even want to come over here and play hoops anymore," Troy said in a rush.

"Whoa . . . whoa," his dad said. "Troy, I hope you're only doing that talent show because you want to do it."

*Want* to do it? Troy thought he *had* to do it! "I get it that hanging with Mr. Evans and the boosters is a really big deal for my future," he said cautiously.

His dad sat down on the bed. Clearly, it was time to set the record straight. "I got carried away talking up shaking hands at Lava Springs. But whatever college turns out to be right for you, scholarship or not, we'll make it work as a family. We've got your back, Troy."

"Yeah?" Troy said, feeling the first ray of hope that he had felt since . . . since Sharpay had started micromanaging his life.

"Bet on it," his dad said. "Here's my only rule about the future: wherever you go, just make sure you don't leave yourself behind."

Troy smiled at his dad as a huge wave of relief swept through his body.

★ ☆ ★

**B**ut when Troy arrived at work the next day, the first thing he noticed was that there was a new lifeguard on duty. And when he walked through the kitchen, he could sense that his friends were uneasy around him.

As the day wore on, it was clear that the only one having fun was Sharpay.

Kelsi played the piano for the lunch crowd without her usual sparkle. Ryan sat by the pool, but even the beautiful day couldn't cheer him up. Taylor walked through the kitchen and noticed how quiet it was.

And Troy just waited for the day to end. Everyone, he knew, was missing Gabriella . . . but nobody missed her more than he did.

Finally, the day was over. Troy hopped in a golf cart, and didn't stop until he got to the middle of the empty course. He took several deep breaths of the night air, stuck a tee in the ground, picked up a golf club, and swung.

The ball sailed through the twilight. Troy watched it go, wondering what had happened to his carefree summer. He thought about how he had fallen in with other people's plans for his future without considering what he wanted to do. And then he made a very important decision.

Things were about to change. From now on, Troy Bolton was going to chart his own course.

# CHAPTER 13

The next morning started out just like any other at Lava Springs Country Club. Club members ate breakfast on the terrace, golfers walked out to the range, and tennis players warmed up their serves.

On the eighteenth hole, a man hunched over his golf club, preparing to make a short putt. But just as he drew the club back to hit the ball, the air was torn by a piercing scream. "WHAT?!!!"

The golfer flinched, knocking his ball off the green.

A tennis player hit her serve into the fence.

In the kitchen, a chef tossed an omelet completely out of the pan.

A diver's beautiful jackknife turned into a clumsy belly flop.

A valet backed a car into a sign advertising the talent show, knocking the sign to the ground.

And on the stage inside the party tent, Sharpay was hyperventilating as Troy stood by.

"What do you mean you're not going to be in my show?" she cried in outraged tones.

"That's exactly it," he said calmly.

Could it be that he just didn't understand the enormity of what he was saying? "We're singing a *duet*, Troy," she explained impatiently. "A duet means two people. Mostly me in this case, but whatever. Duet."

He shrugged. "I'm an employee, and there aren't any employees in the show."

"You're an honorary member," she explained.

"Was," Troy said. "I'm asking Mr. Fulton for my kitchen job back. The memo said they're short-handed on staff for the party."

"Listen to me, there's too much at stake for you

tonight," she said impatiently. "An entire table of university boosters are all coming to see you. Thanks to me."

"Too bad they're going to miss Ryan and the Wildcats," Troy said. "That's worth seeing."

"They're not messing up my show!" she snapped.

"Then neither am I," he said firmly.

"But your parents are coming, too!" she wailed.

"I'll be their waiter," he said. "They'll be thrilled." He turned on his heel and walked off.

Kelsi had watched the whole scene from a corner of the room. Now she watched Troy go, her eyes wide. And Sharpay—Kelsi had never seen her so angry!

She didn't know what this meant, except that it was sure to be a wild night!

That evening, there was a festive air at Lava Springs Country Club as a crowd of members, all dressed in their best, filled the party tent. Chatting happily, they sat down at balloon-decked tables to eat their lavish dinners.

Backstage, Sharpay was dressed in her costume,

trying to make Mr. Fulton see things her way. For once, this wasn't working.

"I cannot order Mr. Bolton to sing," the manager said. "That's not part of his job description." He adjusted the tuxedo he was wearing and added hopefully, "However, as you know I do have a theatrical background, and I think I can still hit a high C, if asked in a pinch. . . ."

"I don't need a high C, I need divine intervention," she snapped. "We have three hundred people arriving." She turned to the club girls. "I thought I told Lea to find Ryan!"

"She did," Ryan said. "Here I am."

"Thank goodness," Sharpay said. "Warm up the volcano. 'Humu Humu' is back in."

"Enjoy your pineapple on your own, Sharpay," Ryan said. "I'm not doing the show."

"What?!" Sharpay gasped. Was *everyone* turning against her? "Get your costume on."

But Ryan shook his head. "I took your advice. I sold it on eBay. You love the spotlight. Guess what? Now it's all yours."

He turned and left, happy to have had—for once—the last word.

Troy hung his golf clothes, carefully wrapped in plastic bags, in his employee locker. He put his golf clubs away. He placed the golf-cart key on the shelf. Then he pulled his name badge off the locker and buttoned his waiter's jacket, ready to go to work.

When he turned around, he found Chad, Zeke, Jason, and Ryan standing behind him with their arms folded.

"Kelsi told us what went down between you and Sharpay," Chad said.

Troy sensed an opening, a chance to make things right with his friends, and he decided to take it. "I'm sorry I messed up your show."

"Yeah, and show business is our entire lives," Zeke said with a grin.

Troy laughed. "I know I've been acting pretty weird. I'm hoping you haven't permanently filled my slot in the two-on-two game. And, Ryan, I know you put a lot of work in with these guys . . . so I apologize."

The guys nodded. All they had wanted was an apology . . . and their old friend Troy back.

"We think you should sing tonight," Chad said.

"What? I already made up my mind," Troy replied.

"All those people are out there," Ryan said persuasively. "You're good. And I don't really want to see my sister crash and burn." He stopped and thought. "At least, I think I don't." He turned to Zeke. "By the way, I hope you hid that pastry cart because when Sharpay gets nervous, she eats."

Sharpay was, in fact, very nervous. She had the pastry cart in her dressing room and was stuffing one dessert after another into her mouth when Mr. Fulton came in.

"I don't want to tell you how to produce your show, but the first three acts haven't exactly lit the house on fire," he said.

"I'm ruined," she said through a mouthful of éclair. "My life is over! I've been a good girl. I've never lied, except when necessary. I've always bought my parents expensive gifts—using their

253

credit card, of course. But I don't deserve this humiliation. . . ."

Mr. Fulton decided it was time to interrupt this aria of self-pity. "At the very least, you'd better get out there and sing. It's either you or Mrs. Hoffenfeffer and her talking sock puppet."

"Take me now, God," Sharpay said.

"I think I remember my old soft shoe," Mr. Fulton said eagerly. "I'll give it a try. But you better warm up those vocal cords."

He left, and Sharpay slumped in front of her dressing-room mirror. She caught sight of her reflection: her hair was a mess, her face was smeared with frosting, and, worst of all, she looked like what she was: a girl who had manipulated everyone to get what she wanted.

"What would Madonna do in this situation?" she asked herself. After a moment's thought, she said, "Okay, forget that."

As she stared bleakly into the mirror, she saw Troy reflected behind her. She whirled around.

"How's your show going?" he asked.

"How's it going?" She sighed and admitted, "My

show makes the captain of the Titanic look like he won the lottery."

He hesitated, then said, "I'll sing with you, Sharpay."

She stared at him, incredulous. "What?"

"I did promise to sing with you, and I keep my promises," he explained. "But what was that thing you said to me when I first started working here?"

She cast her mind back. "Bring me an iced tea?"

He smiled a little. "Think harder." He prompted her, "We're—"

She paused, then said, "All in this together."

"Yeah, that." Troy waited for her to connect the dots.

"Well . . . we are, so let's get out there and knock 'em dead, Troy Bolton!" she said brightly.

He sighed as he realized that he was going to have to explain this. "But not just you and me, Sharpay. The Wildcats, too. I do the show . . . if the Wildcats do the show." He glanced over at the demolished slices of cheesecake, coconut cake, and apple torte. "Or do you just want to sit here and polish off what's left of the pastry cart?"

Outside the door, Kelsi was listening intently.

Sharpay thought about the mess of a show that was happening right now onstage. She looked at the mirror and saw the mess she had become. And then she looked at Troy.

"I just sort of wish you were doing this . . . for me," she said, sincere for the first time. "You're a good guy, Troy. . . . Actually, right now I think I like you better than I like myself." Startled, she looked at him with wide eyes. "Did I say that?"

He grinned, realizing for the first time that maybe Sharpay was someone he could actually be friends with.

# ♪ CHAPTER 14 ♪

**W**ord spread through the Wildcats' ranks that they were going to be in the show! Chad jumped on a bus cart and flew backstage, picking Taylor up on the way. Jason and Kelsi came running out of the kitchen, with Zeke right behind them.

Ryan grabbed Troy as he ran by and said, "Sharpay wants to do a different song. Kelsi will work it out with you."

"What? But . . ." Troy was already nervous, and now he was supposed to sing a completely different song?

Ryan nodded reassuringly. "Just go with it."

"Where's Chad and Taylor?" Troy asked.

Kelsi grabbed Troy and pulled him to her piano to practice. They didn't have time for Troy to be nervous or to ask questions, she thought. After all, they didn't want to spoil the surprise. . . .

While the excitement was building at the country club, Gabriella was lying on her bed reading a book.

Suddenly, Chad and Taylor burst into her room. Taylor went to her closet and began pulling out dresses.

Gabriella sat up, shocked. "What are you—"

"Yell at us in the car," Chad said briefly.

She shook her head, confused. "Why aren't you working?"

Taylor grinned at her. "We are."

Gabriella's lips tightened. "I'm not going back to the club," she said firmly.

"Explain that to Ryan," Taylor suggested. "Our show's back in, and he said nothing will work without you. Trust me, he's right."

Gabriella hesitated. Taylor and Chad exchanged a look of satisfaction.

Gabriella was in.

A magician was onstage, performing his tricks.

Troy's parents watched the act with a mixture of amazement and dismay as they ate their dinner.

"What do you think?" Mr. Bolton asked.

"Well . . . it's nothing I've ever seen before," his wife said.

"Keep smiling," he replied.

She rolled her eyes. "That's the easy part."

While Sharpay sat backstage doing vocal exercises, Mr. Fulton took the microphone.

"And now, ladies and gentlemen, I've been handed a change in the program," he said. "I'm not quite sure what to expect, but, as they say, the show must go on. . . ."

Kelsi ran onstage to sit at the piano while a flurry of activity went on in the wings.

"Why'd you switch songs?" Troy asked Sharpay. "I don't know if I can pull this off."

She looked at him with an expression of shocked surprise. "Switched songs? WHAT?"

He met her look with one of confusion. "Yeah. Ryan said . . ."

Onstage, Mr. Fulton was saying, "So, here's our assistant golf pro, Troy Bolton . . ."

Kelsi began playing. Troy gulped, but he went onstage and began singing.

Sharpay spotted Ryan. "How am I supposed to get through this?" she asked. "I don't know this song."

"I know," he said simply.

She looked at him for a puzzled moment, then realized what was happening just as the back curtain opened to reveal all the Wildcats. They moved aside and Gabriella stepped onto the stage, singing along with Troy.

And here they were, back where they had started . . . Troy and Gabriella, singing for a roomful of people but with eyes only for each other. They performed the song sweetly and simply and, as it gradually built to the finish, it seemed clear that this was a song about two voices that were meant to be together.

When they finished, there was a moment of silence, then the ballroom burst into applause. Troy hugged Gabriella.

Caught up in the spirit of the evening, Sharpay grabbed the microphone and introduced Ryan and the Wildcats. Ryan cued Kelsi, who began playing—and before anyone could blink, the Wildcats had turned the entire ballroom into their stage! They were singing about being friends and believing in each other. And when the song ended, the entire room erupted into a huge celebration!

In the midst of it all, Troy's dad found him and said, "I thought you told me you weren't having fun here. Could have fooled me."

Troy grinned, but before he could reply, Sharpay's dad came up to them. "I've been talking to the committee," he said. "It's pretty much unanimous. Doesn't matter what happens on court next year. We want Troy at U of A. Full boat. Just the kind of kid we want on campus."

Troy's mouth dropped open. It was beyond anything he had dreamed of—but it was happening awfully fast . . . and he didn't know what to say.

"Well, Troy will need to think about his options," Mr. Bolton said easily, rescuing him. "Too early to tell. Summer's just starting."

Troy glanced at his dad and smiled. There would be time enough to think about the future—*after* he'd had the best summer ever.

Then, Mr. Fulton stepped back onstage, holding the Star Dazzle award.

"Ladies and gentlemen, the winner of this year's Star Dazzle award is, of course, our one and only—"

Before he could finish, Sharpay grabbed the microphone and said, "Mr. Ryan Evans!"

She took the award from Mr. Fulton and handed it to a shocked but beaming Ryan, then she turned to find that Zeke was standing in front of her and holding out a pastry.

"Chocolate éclair?" she cried. "How did you know that was my favorite?"

"Wild guess," he grinned. "Maybe it was the three you ate before the show? But there are more on the way."

★ ☆ ★

It had been a night to remember—and the fun only continued the next day, when the club was closed for an employees-only party. Everyone—including Sharpay!—hung out at the pool. They even sang and danced a little.

Later that night, the Wildcats were lying on the golf course, enjoying the afterglow of their triumph.

"Man, what a party!" Troy exclaimed.

"Glad we don't have to clean it up," Chad said.

"Actually," Taylor said, "I think we do."

Gabriella smiled dreamily. "But not until tomorrow."

Zeke nodded. "When we're back on the clock and getting paid," he added pointedly.

After a small pause, Sharpay said, "I'll help."

Every head snapped in her direction. Everyone was shocked—but no one was more shocked than Sharpay.

"Did I say that?" she asked.

Suddenly, the sprinklers all began spraying water everywhere. There were joyous shrieks as the Wildcats got thoroughly soaked. They started racing across the grass, laughing.

But Troy and Gabriella hung back a little, and gazed at each other. It felt like everything was right again. Caught up in the moment, they leaned in and at last they kissed tenderly. The night couldn't have been more perfect. Smiling at each other, they ran after their friends under the starry summer sky.

PRESENTING

Disney

# HIGH SCHOOL MUSICAL 3 SENIOR YEAR

EAST HIGH

ROCK

STAR

LOST IN MUSIC

The Junior Novel
Adapted by N. B. Grace

Based on the screenplay written by Peter Barsocchini
Based on characters created by Peter Barsocchini
Executive Producer Kenny Ortega
Produced by Bill Borden and Barry Rosenbush
Directed by Kenny Ortega

# CHAPTER 1

The East High gym was rocking as the first half of the grudge match between the East High Wildcats and the West High Knights was coming to a close. The cheerleaders for both basketball teams were leading the audience in cheers, and the East High band's drummers were pounding out a beat. But on the court, the players didn't pay attention to any sounds except their own breathing and occasional grunting as they blocked shots, jumped for rebounds, and raced across the floor.

In the middle of all the chaos, Wildcats captain

Troy Bolton took a deep breath, pushed his hair out of his eyes, and glanced at the scoreboard.

The score was twenty-four for the Wildcats . . . and thirty-seven for the Knights.

Suddenly, the buzzer rang.

The first half of the game was over.

And the Wildcats were getting crushed.

As the team members piled into the locker room, their faces looked shell-shocked. Several players took a seat on the benches. They slumped over, exhausted. Others leaned on their lockers, trying not to look discouraged.

Every player's eyes turned to look at Troy. He was sitting near his best friend, the team's co-captain, Chad Danforth. Two other seniors, Zeke Baylor and Jason Cross, stood a few feet away. Troy seemed unaware of the others' anxiety. His piercing blue eyes were completely focused on the dry-erase board that had been set up at the end of the locker room.

Coach Bolton, who was Troy's father, looked around the room. He knew how his team was feeling. And he knew he had to get them back on track. He was confident that they could come from behind in the second half. He reached out with an eraser and wiped the play diagrams off the board.

The coach looked at his teammates intently. "We've dug ourselves a hole, and the only way out is on each other's shoulders," he said firmly.

Coach Bolton continued. "No more X's and O's," he told the team. "Forget the scoreboard. Here's the number that means something. . . ." He reached out and scribbled "16" on the board. "Sixteen minutes left in the game . . . the season . . . and for the seniors on this squad"—he glanced over at Troy, Chad, Zeke, and Jason—"sixteen minutes left in a Wildcats uniform."

He gave Troy and Chad a serious look. "Captains?"

Troy stood up. This was the moment when he had to rally the Wildcats and raise their spirits. Fortunately, he wasn't alone. "Hey, you heard Coach. The sixteen minutes are going to stay with us for a long time after we leave East High . . . so it's now or never," he said. "Chad?" he asked, glancing over at his co-captain.

As Troy expected, Chad jumped up and stood

next to him. He looked over at the other Wildcats and smiled.

"What team?" he cheered enthusiastically.

The players grinned. They could always count on Troy and Chad to raise their spirits. "Wildcats!" they yelled back in unison.

"What team?" Chad shouted even louder.

"WILDCATS!" This time, their shouts rattled the roof.

Chad stepped forward and held out his right hand. Once more, he cried out, "What team?"

Nine hands joined his in the middle of a circle. "Wildcats!" everyone cheered.

Their hands flew into the air, and then the teammates burst out of the locker room into the Hallway of Champions and headed back to the gym. After Troy's pep talk and Chad's rousing cheer, they were totally fired up.

Maybe, Troy thought, a little *too* fired up . . .

He stopped at the door to the gym and turned to face his teammates. "Yo, one other thing—"

Everyone turned to look at him.

"Did anyone actually *wash* their lucky socks?" Troy asked, giving them all a serious stare. "The same socks we've worn for three straight playoff games . . . games we *won*?"

Small smiles appeared on everyone's faces as soon as they realized what Troy's question was leading up to.

"Mine never left my locker all season," Chad said proudly.

"I kept mine in my lunch bag," Jason added.

Troy nodded, satisfied. "Zeke?"

"I vacuum-packed mine," Zeke said with a laugh.

Troy grinned. "That's what I'm talking about!"

The tension eased as everyone burst out laughing. Now we're ready to play, Troy thought with satisfaction as he threw open the doors, and the team ran back out to center court.

The Wildcats knew one thing as the second half of the game started—like Troy said, it was now or never. If they wanted to win, they had to go full throttle. And from the moment they hit the floor, that's what they did.

Troy was everywhere, motioning for his teammates to follow the plays they'd practiced for months. Chad passed the ball and ran toward the net, ready to dunk a basket for two points.

The game raged on, and the Wildcats kept piling up points. Coach Bolton paced intensely on the sidelines, matched step for step by the West High coach, who was walking up and down the sidelines on the other side of the court. The East High cheerleaders, led by Martha Cox, pulled out their best cheers to pump up the team.

In the bleachers, Gabriella Montez was watching anxiously. The Wildcats were catching up, but time was ticking away. Would they actually be able to pull off a victory?

As the scoreboard counted off the seconds, the action got even more heated, and Troy was knocked to the ground, causing the referee to call a foul against West High. Stunned, Troy looked around the gym at the crowd yelling, the cheerleaders leaping into the air . . . and then he found Gabriella in the sea of faces. Her eyes met his and, just like that, he was back in the game.

He stepped up to the line and sank two free throws with ease.

The crowd erupted in cheers. It was anyone's game now.

On the sidelines, Coach Bolton rapidly sketched a play. The team ran over and the coach told them what they needed to do.

Troy nodded toward the end of the bench, where Jimmie "the Rocket" Zara was sitting. Jimmie's friend, Donny Dion, was sitting next to him. They were both sophomores new to the team, and a little in awe of being in a championship game.

The coach smiled to himself. He and Troy had had exactly the same thought.

"Jimmie Z, you're in!" Coach Bolton yelled.

The other Wildcats exchanged shocked glances, but no one was more surprised than Jimmie. He was so surprised, in fact, that he ripped off his warm-up jacket too fast and ended up removing his jersey as well. As the crowd around him chuckled, the coach gathered his team into a huddle.

Across the court, the West High Knights were staring at the Wildcats with determination. They wanted the championship trophy as badly as the Wildcats did.

But Troy didn't even notice. He was too focused on what he had to do. Next to him, Jimmie was bouncing on his toes, filled with energy and trying to settle his nerves.

"Save it for the game, Rocketman," Troy said. "And keep your eyes on me."

And then they were back in the action for the last play. . . .

As the ref blew his whistle, the Wildcats all leaned down to touch their lucky socks. Then they were on the court, running the decoy play they had practiced so many times.

Chad threw the ball in bounds to Zeke, who fired it right back at Chad. Troy was surrounded by three players for the Knights, but he managed to slip free and grab a shovel pass from Chad. He set up for a jump shot and every person in the gym looked at the basket . . . except for Troy.

Instead of taking the shot, he passed the ball to Jimmie, who was completely unguarded. Jimmie hesitated for a split second, then made a layup for two points just as the buzzer sounded.

The fake had worked!

The Wildcats had won!

Fans poured onto the gym floor, cheering and giving each other high fives. The Wildcats mascot joined them and pulled off the head to his costume. It was none other than Ryan Evans, grinning broadly as he joined in the celebration.

Troy's teammates lifted him onto their shoulders, and the championship trophy was passed up to him.

Once again, his eyes found Gabriella's in the crowd, and he grinned. Then he lifted the trophy high in the air in celebration.

Troy's and Chad's mothers were putting the last touches on a spread of food when the two boys burst into the Boltons' kitchen. Chad grabbed his mom and gave her an exuberant hug.

"So . . . what'd you think of the game?" he asked, smiling.

She gave him a loving squeeze back. "Did you have to take it down to the buzzer? I was a nervous wreck!" she exclaimed.

277

Troy spun his own mother around before hugging her also.

"Back-to-back championships!" he yelled. Last year, he didn't think anything could top the feeling of the Wildcats winning the district championship. *Now*, of course, there was something better—winning two in a row!

"Fantastic!" his mom exclaimed. She put on a mock motherly voice. "But you're still helping us clean up after the party."

Troy and Chad glanced over at Zeke, who was also in the kitchen. He was still wearing his Wildcats uniform but had added a chef's hat and an apron. He was carefully putting icing on an array of basketball-shaped cupcakes.

As Chad reached out to snag one, Zeke playfully slapped his hand away. "They're cooling. I'll let you know when they're ready!" Zeke exclaimed, laughing. "Out of my kitchen, mister!"

As more Wildcats made their way from the game to the Boltons' house, the party began picking up steam. Troy maneuvered his way in between a barbecue grill, a spirited game of Ping-Pong, and groups of kids dancing, his eyes searching for Gabriella.

Finally, there was a break in the crowd and he found her. He gave Gabriella a broad smile and reached for her hand. "Hey! Fix you a plate?" he offered.

Gabriella inhaled and smelled the spicy, mouthwatering barbecue, heard the sizzle of hamburgers on the grill, and eyed the spread of side dishes being laid out. "One of everything," she said with a grin.

But just then, Chad, Troy's dad, and Coach Kellog, the University of Albuquerque basketball coach, walked over to them. Gabriella politely stepped aside.

Coach Bolton was beaming with pride. "Coach Kellog, you got any empty lockers up at U of A?"

The college coach looked over at Troy and Chad. "Not for long, I hope," he said with a smile.

Just then, Chad's father walked up to them. Coach Bolton threw an arm around his shoulder and motioned to Coach Kellog.

"I bet Charlie Danforth will suit up for you next season, too, if you just ask him," Troy's dad joked.

Mr. Danforth grinned. "A front-row seat will do just fine," he said.

"Well, the kind of team play I saw tonight goes a long way with me," Coach Kellog commented.

Troy and Chad exchanged high fives while their dads looked on proudly.

Coach Kellog gave Troy and Chad an inquisitive look. "And we're counting on seeing you both in Redhawk uniforms next season, right?"

"Done deal," Chad replied, nodding his head.

"Amen to that, son!" Chad's father cheered.

Troy smiled weakly, then excused himself as soon as he could. He wandered around the backyard and craned his neck, searching for Gabriella again. He spotted her on the other side of the yard and started heading in her direction, but only managed to take a few steps before being intercepted by Jimmie Zara, whose face was beaming with excitement.

"Dude, great house!" Jimmie shouted. "Your room is *way* cool."

Troy raised his eyebrows. "You were in my room?"

Jimmie nodded proudly. "I took a picture. Look."

He held up his digital camera so Troy could see the tiny screen.

As Troy looked at the photo of his bedroom, Jimmie added, "I'm doing mine the same way."

"Wow," Troy commented, unsure about how to react. *Or about how to escape.* "That's great, Jimmie."

Just then, Troy had an idea. "Oh, man, I left the championship trophy in my truck . . . I hope it's still there. . . ."

"Don't worry, I'm on it!" Jimmie exclaimed. He quickly headed in the direction of Troy's truck.

Troy shook his head. Then he started to look for Gabriella, again.

Gabriella was leaning against a tree, gazing up at the stars. She loved her friends, she loved parties, she loved celebrating a Wildcats win . . . but sometimes she just needed some time to herself.

She sighed happily. It was such a beautiful night. The only thing that would make it better was—

Suddenly, a hand grabbed her arm and pulled her behind the tree.

Gabriella found herself staring up into Troy's blue eyes. He smiled down at her and motioned toward the two plates of food he had brought over. "One of everything," he said. "Your wish is my command. Now follow me."

He headed across the lawn, trying to keep both plates steady. Gabriella followed, grinning as she saw him nearly drop a plate, then recover with the grace of a champion basketball player. A few minutes later, she found herself perched high above the party in a tree house. Troy was sitting next to her with their picnic spread out before them.

"Another top secret hiding place?" Gabriella asked in a teasing voice.

"You are the second girl ever allowed up here," Troy said solemnly.

Gabriella raised one eyebrow at his comment.

He grinned. "The other was my mom, and she only climbed up to get me down. I haven't been up here since I was ten. . . ."

His voice trailed off. Gabriella gave him a questioning look.

He smiled and confessed, "Okay . . . thirteen."

She continued looking at him.

"All right," he admitted, "last week. When I was nervous about the game."

Gabriella smiled. "Well, I'm honored," she replied. "*And* ready for these . . ." she said, motioning to a plate of cupcakes. They each grabbed one.

"Was that the coach from U of A down there?" Gabriella asked, turning serious.

Troy nodded.

"I bet he's already got your name on a locker," she commented.

Troy's smile waned a bit. They both looked down at the party that was still in full swing below them. Gabriella's mother had now arrived and was chatting with Troy's parents. Troy sighed as he watched his dad's face, which was lit up with happiness over the Wildcats' win—and, Troy knew, his son's future.

Troy sighed. "Yeah, it's always been my dad's dream that I end up at his alma mater," he said.

Gabriella nodded. "My mom and I have been talking about Stanford University ever since I was born," she said.

"And you're already accepted," Troy said, trying to sound encouraging. "That's so cool."

"Except my mom *won't* stop talking about it," she admitted. "It's embarrassing."

"She's proud of you," Troy said. He paused, then added, "So am I. Everyone is."

Gabriella looked down. It was nice that everyone was proud of her, but . . .

She looked at Troy seriously. "The thing about Stanford is that it's a thousand and . . ."

Together, they both said, "Fifty-three miles—"

"From here," Troy finished the sentence. "I know. And now the rest of the school year is coming at us so fast."

There was a moment's silence. Then Gabriella said, "I wish it would all just . . . stop. At least, slow down."

Troy knew what she meant. Here they were, just months away from leaving home for the first time and being on their own . . . it was exciting. But kind of scary. Troy knew the time that they had together before the summer was over was incredibly important. He could see by the look in Gabriella's eyes that she felt the same way.

Suddenly, they were interrupted by a loud

voice. "Troy, you have guests!" Mrs. Bolton's voice called out.

She peered more closely at the tree house, then smiled and added, "Hi, Gabriella!"

Troy and Gabriella exchanged rueful glances. They'd much rather stay in the tree house, just the two of them. But they knew that would be rude.

So, sighing, they both climbed down the tree house ladder to join the party.

# CHAPTER 2

The next morning, buses started arriving at East High School, releasing dozens of students into a new day. Other students arrived on bikes or skateboards, or had walked to school, taking advantage of the beautiful day. All of them were greeted by a new banner across the front of the building that said, CONGRATULATIONS WILDCATS BACK-TO-BACK CHAMPIONS!

The students who drove to school were angling for good spots in the parking lot. All except one. A shiny, pink convertible Mustang rode right past the student spaces and into a private spot out-lined in pink right in front of the school. Sharpay Evans, Ryan's twin sister and co-president of the Drama Club, stepped out, the heels of her pink boots clattering on the pavement. But before she had taken even a few steps, two freshmen jumped forward with buckets and rags and began washing her already spotless car.

The school doors seemed to sweep open on their own as Sharpay headed inside, her long, blond hair swishing behind her. She strode down the hall without looking right or left. She didn't need to—the other students parted to make way for her, bumping into each other to get out of her path.

She breezed past a pedestal in the lobby just as Chad placed the Wildcats' new championship trophy on top of it. Troy, Zeke, and Jason grinned as the other students congratulated them.

Sharpay glanced at the group casually. "Hi, Troy," she said. "When's the big game?"

Troy gave her a curious look. "Yesterday," he said slowly.

Sharpay looked up from checking her text messages. "Well, good luck," she replied. She continued walking down the hall.

The members of the basketball team stared after her in disbelief. How could she not know that they had played the game, that they had won, that they were champs . . . ?

But Sharpay, as usual, was totally focused on herself. She got to her locker, which was twice the size of everyone else's and painted her signature shade of pink. She glanced around to make sure no one was watching as she opened her combination lock. Suddenly she jumped, startled to find a bookish young girl with her hair pulled back, and wearing a white blouse, standing only inches away from her.

"What are *you*?" Sharpay asked. "I mean," she corrected herself, "*who* are you?"

"Good morning, Miss Evans," the girl answered. She had a crisp British accent and a very respectful manner. "I'm Tiara Gold. I've just transferred to East High from London and noticed on the board that you were in need of a personal assistant?"

Sharpay nodded. "Well, with finals, prom, and

graduation, I need someone tracking my appointments and assignments," she said grandly. "Most important, I need someone to run lines with me for the spring musical."

Sharpay then paused. Sometimes she forgot that civilians didn't know how theater people talked. She added regally, "That's a theater term for—"

"Learning your role," Tiara finished. "I understand."

She reached past Sharpay and began to rearrange her locker, which came equipped with a pullout wardrobe rack and custom-built shelves.

"It's best to keep science and math together, since those are your first classes of the day," Tiara explained briskly.

Sharpay looked at her suspiciously and frowned. "How do you know my schedule?"

"I took the liberty of checking, simply to make certain I'd have your nonfat, no-foam soy latte ready for free period," Tiara replied. She handed Sharpay her beverage.

Sharpay's frown disappeared. "One packet of sweetener," she told Tiara.

Tiara nodded. "Organic, of course."

Sharpay raised an eyebrow. She was impressed. "I'll e-mail you my wardrobe choices each morning so that our outfits won't clash." Not that they would, Sharpay thought to herself. She doubted that Tiara had anything fabulous and pink in her closet.

She handed Tiara her book bag, relieved that she had finally found someone who clearly understood the many burdens of fame and popularity. As she walked down the hallway, it occurred to Sharpay that she should say something nice to Tiara, maybe pay her a little compliment to let her know she was appreciated. After all, weren't the biggest stars always the nicest—*especially* when it came to the little people?

She turned her head and quickly added, "By the way, I like the accent."

Then she tossed her hair and walked away.

Troy was just about to go into homeroom. It was hard to believe, he thought, that in only a few months he would never enter Ms. Darbus's homeroom again. All of a sudden, Jimmie popped up out of nowhere. Troy jumped, surprised by the sophomore's sudden appearance, but Jimmie didn't seem to notice.

Jimmie gave Troy an excited grin. "Troy, my brother, can I have your gym locker?" he asked.

Troy's mouth dropped open. "What?" He hadn't even graduated yet, and Jimmie was already moving in on his locker?!

"Like . . . starting next week?" Jimmie suggested. "It'll help me with the guys next season if you do that."

"Why didn't I think of that?" Troy commented under his breath. Just then, the bell rang.

"Oh, man!" Jimmie cried, a panicked look on his face. "Another tardy!" He went racing down the hall.

Shaking his head, Troy went into homeroom, where the other Wildcats were already taking their seats. As Chad passed Ms. Darbus, he handed over his basketball with the resigned air of someone who has spent four years under her strict rule. She took it without a word and placed it on a special perch beside her desk, then continued distributing the printouts she was holding.

Sharpay ran into the room in a huff. When she turned to take a seat, she found Tiara right on her heels. Although she was impressed by Tiara's devotion, Sharpay realized she hadn't been quite clear about her duties. "Oh, you can go now," she said haughtily, waving a hand in dismissal.

To her surprise, Tiara didn't instantly obey this command. "I managed to transfer into your homeroom," she explained. "Just in case I could be of service."

Sharpay gave Tiara a long, considering look. "Some people might be freaked out by you," she said. "Me . . . I like it. Take a seat."

As the students gradually took their places, still talking, Ms. Darbus called the class to order. "All right, settle down. I know we're all still excited about the Wildcats' top-to-bottom championship. . . ."

"That would be back-to-back, Miss D!" Chad called out.

Ms. Darbus sighed loudly. "In *any* case, it was a grand slam. Well done."

Troy and Chad rolled their eyes at the use of a *baseball* term to refer to their *basketball* triumph.

Ms. Darbus continued. "Now, student body president and co-editor of the yearbook, Taylor McKessie, has important announcements," she said. "Taylor?"

Immediately, Taylor stood up from her desk, grabbed a pointer, and slid a dry-erase board in front of the class. She pointed to each item written on the board in turn and said, without taking a breath, "Senior-trip subcommittee meets tomorrow and reports Thursday to prom committee, headed by Martha . . . Pick up your prom tickets from her. Graduation committee convenes Monday, following yearbook planning. Picture deadline is Thursday. Finals study groups alternate with *all* of the above. Questions?"

The class stared at her in stunned silence. Finally, Chad piped up. "What's the lunch special in the cafeteria today?" he asked jokingly.

"New York Deli," Taylor answered in a serious tone. "Anyone else?"

"Moving on," Ms. Darbus interrupted, taking the pointer away. "Sharpay Evans, four-term Drama Club co-President . . . spring musical report?" she asked.

Sharpay nodded. "With prom, finals, and everyone being so busy, we'll select something very modest to perform. Perhaps even a one-woman show."

Ms. Darbus noticed that Kelsi Nielsen was scribbling furiously in her notebook. "A little light on the sign-ups, Kelsi?" she inquired.

Kelsi barely looked up and continued writing in her notebook. "Oh, no, actually we're doing pretty well. . . ."

Ms. Darbus walked over to Kelsi and grabbed her clipboard. "Well, well, well . . . almost the entire homeroom. How inspiring!" she exclaimed.

Everyone in the class turned to look at each other, puzzled. They didn't *remember* signing up for the spring musical auditions.

Sharpay's mouth dropped open in disbelief. She thought she'd made it clear last year that no one should ever again consider encroaching on her territory, which was the theater and every-thing that took place in it.

Every eye turned toward Kelsi, who lowered the brim of her hat and slid down in her seat.

"So, I'll be seeing all of you during free period

to discuss the show," Ms. Darbus went on, unaware of the tension in the room. "*And* for a *very* special announcement—"

As usual, Ms. Darbus's timing was perfect. The bell rang before anyone could respond. Everybody began gathering their notebooks to head for their next class. As Chad passed Ms. Darbus, she handed him back his basketball.

Troy sighed. "Leave it to Darbus to make free period mandatory."

**W**hen the bell rang announcing free period, Sharpay was the first person at the theater and onstage. She was pacing back and forth. A protesting crowd of Wildcats surrounded Kelsi, who was sitting at the piano.

"I'll be retaking my finals two or three times. I'm moving into the library," Jason told her.

"Kels, I was going to be using free period to work on my truck," Troy said.

"I've got five new recipes to nail for my Family Science final," Zeke added.

Taylor looked over at Gabriella. "We've got a yearbook to edit. So no can do."

Kelsi looked crestfallen. "Sorry," she said quietly. "I just thought since it was the last show, everyone would want to do it."

Gabriella hadn't yet said anything. She chose this moment to step forward. "Hey, listen up. Kelsi's right. We should do this." She looked around at her friends. "Jason—Taylor, Martha, and I can help you study. Zeke—we're your official tasters. This is our last chance to do something together, all of us. Something really fun."

From her spot at center stage, Sharpay had been following the debate with interest and delight. So no one wants to be in the musical, she thought, smiling to herself. But now, she could tell that Gabriella's emotional appeal was working. She frowned.

"Oh, yippie," she muttered under her breath. She could just imagine it: friendship and fun and high spirits . . . in *her* theater! Where there was supposed to be drama and discipline and one—count her, *one*—diva!

Still, there was a chance that Gabriella's argument might fail. Taylor, for example, seemed skeptical.

"But how much time will it take?" Taylor asked.

"And what is the show about?" Chad questioned.

A voice from somewhere behind them said, "You, Mr. Danforth."

They turned to see Ms. Darbus, holding her clipboard, striding down the aisle toward them. "The spring musical," she said grandly, "is all about . . . *you.*"

"*Me?*" Chad sounded surprised—and alarmed.

He wasn't the only one.

Up on the stage, Sharpay fainted.

**W**hen Sharpay came to a few moments later, she found that Tiara was gently spritzing her face with a spray bottle filled with mineral water to revive her. She sat up groggily.

Ms. Darbus, who knew a hysterical faint when she saw one, continued without missing a beat. "It's about *all* of you. And all of you will create it . . . a show about your last days at East High. We'll call it"—she paused dramatically, as if trying to find the perfect name—"*Senior Year.*"

The Wildcats looked at each other. *Senior Year? That* was the name of their musical?

Chad shrugged and kept spinning his basket-ball. He didn't care *what* the musical was called. All he cared about was not getting onstage and singing. *Ever.*

"Kelsi will compose, Ryan choreograph . . . and I'll do my best to guide you," Ms. Darbus announced, trying to sound modest.

She then looked at the group intently. "Now, important news from The Juilliard School in New York City, America's preeminent college for the performing arts. Yes, for the first time in East High history, four of you are being considered for one available theater arts scholarship." She looked at the seniors proudly.

She held up a letter. "Yes, Juilliard is consider-ing Miss Sharpay Evans . . ."

Sharpay beamed. "I'm already packed."

Ms. Darbus continued, "Mr. Ryan Evans . . ."

Ryan did a blazing five-second tap dance out of sheer joy.

"Miss Kelsi Nielsen . . ."

Kelsi's eyes opened wide with shock. "Whoa," she said softly. "They got my letter."

"Indeed they did," Ms. Darbus said, smiling. "And finally . . . Mr. Troy Bolton."

Every head swiveled to stare at Troy. He grinned back. After all, this was all a big joke . . . wasn't it?

"Juilliard will send representatives to observe our spring show. So . . . good luck to our four applicants," Ms. Darbus said.

The Drama Club teacher didn't sound like she was joking, but Troy was laughing as he asked his friends, "All right . . . who's the big comedian?" He pointed to Gabriella. "Ha, ha, ha."

Gabriella shrugged. She was as surprised as he was.

Troy turned to Chad. "Pretty good, dude."

But Chad just shook his head. He loved jokes, and this was a good one. He would have been proud to call it his own, except for one thing—he had nothing to do with it.

"Is there something wrong?" Ms. Darbus was a little disappointed at Troy's reaction.

"I didn't apply," he explained. "I've never heard of . . . Juilliard."

"Well, that may be, Mr. Bolton," she said crisply. "But, evidently, Juilliard has heard of *you*."

She focused her attention back to the spring musical. Her gaze swept the group standing in front of her. "And as you create this show, then you must dig down and think about your aspirations, your dreams for the future. Line up, please. Let's begin with Mr. Danforth."

Chad looked at Ms. Darbus blankly. Was she seriously asking Chad what his dreams were? He had only had the same dream since he was ten years old, and everyone knew what it was. Chad spun his basketball to give Ms. Darbus a clue. "My dreams? U of A. Hoops all the way."

Ms. Darbus smiled. "Miss McKessie?"

"*My* future?" Taylor asked. "I'd like to be president of the United States." She paused, smiling happily at the daydream that constantly ran through her mind—whenever she wasn't studying, of course.

"Do we get extra credit for just . . . like . . . showing up?" Jason wanted to know.

Ms. Darbus quietly groaned and turned to

Kelsi, waiting for her response to the question.

"To write some songs we'll remember . . ." she replied wistfully.

Just then, Martha came hurrying into the theater.

"Martha Cox, you're late!" Ms. Darbus shouted.

Martha tried to catch her breath. "I had my American Folk Dance class . . . and thought maybe we could use a few more dancers. . . ."

"I'm feeling a show already!" Ms. Darbus exclaimed, her eyes sparkling with excitement. "Troy Bolton?"

But Troy wasn't in a theatrical mood. "To bust whoever signed me up for this!" he said loudly.

Ms. Darbus sighed. "And Miss Montez?" she asked.

"I think we should stage the perfect prom," Gabriella replied.

Sharpay rolled her eyes. "That's *adorable*," she commented. "What do *I* want? Gosh, I wouldn't know where to begin . . . but I know where it ends." She imagined herself stepping into a spotlight. "Center stage, a single spotlight . . . a huge marquee that reads—"

She swept her hand through the air. No one had any doubts about what she was seeing.

Her name. In lights.

But by lunchtime, the only marquee was the one in the cafeteria. And the only words on it were NEW YORK DELI PLATTER, which meant corned beef on rye, Swiss cheese, potato salad, pickles, and a "Big Apple" parfait, the dessert of the day. In addition to the lunch menu, the sign said, PICK UP YOUR PROM TICKETS TODAY!

Sharpay and Ryan stood in line with their lunch trays. When it was Ryan's turn to order, he said, "I'll have the New York Deli Platter, please, double cheese. And throw in that "Big Apple" parfait . . . if they make it there, I'll eat it anywhere."

Sharpay gave her brother a disapproving look. "How can you think about food at a time like *this*?" she demanded.

"Maybe because it's lunchtime," Ryan suggested.

"I'm talking about the show, Ryan!" Sharpay barked.

Sharpay led the way to the second level of

the cafeteria, with Tiara behind them, carrying Sharpay's lunch tray. As they walked, Sharpay continued talking. "That puppy dog Troy Bolton *pretended* to know nothing about Juilliard." She gave a small snort.

Sharpay and Ryan sat in their usual spot, which was empty and waiting for them thanks to the pink RESERVED sign displayed on the table. Tiara began setting Sharpay's place as Ryan said, "Troy looked genuinely surprised."

"Oh, so the theater fairy *magically* sent in Troy's application?" Sharpay scoffed. "Performers can't fool me, Ryan. They're deceitful, ambitious, and ruthless."

Ryan took a bite of his sandwich and chewed thoughtfully. Then he asked, "Aren't *we* . . . performers?"

Sharpay nodded, glad that Ryan had grasped her point. "Exactly!" she exclaimed.

She said it with such conviction, such absolute, unshakeable faith in their destiny, that Ryan couldn't help but be swayed. Sharpay was right! he thought. They *both* belonged at Juilliard—no matter what it took to get there.

He suddenly frowned as he remembered one important minor detail.

"Wait a minute . . . Ms. D. said there's only one scholarship available," Ryan pointed out.

Sharpay waved one hand dismissively. "We're twins," she said. "They'll have to take us both."

Ryan tried to understand this logic, but Sharpay was already moving on to the first step in her scheme. "Kelsi always writes her best songs for Troy and Gabriella," she said. "So you make certain we get those songs."

"How?" he asked.

"Polish her glasses. Buy her some ruby slippers," Sharpay snapped impatiently. "I don't know. Just do it!"

## CHAPTER 3

"**C**oming to rehearsal today?" Gabriella asked Taylor the next morning as they got off the bus in front of school.

Taylor rolled her eyes. "Do I have a choice? You got us into this." She gave Gabriella a puzzled look. "Which I don't understand. Have you even told *anyone* you're up for Stanford's freshman honors program?"

Gabriella shook her head. Only her mother and Taylor knew that she might be able to start college early—even before she graduated from high school. Not only had she not told anyone else, but she was trying to forget all about the possibility herself.

"You're going to be hearing from them any day," Taylor told her.

Gabriella looked down. "I already heard from them," she admitted.

Just then, Gabriella's cell phone rang, and Troy's face appeared on the screen. She answered the call. "Look up," he said.

"Huh?" Gabriella tilted her head back and blinked in astonishment. Troy was waving from the rooftop of the school!

"Gotta go!" Gabriella told Taylor, hurrying away.

Taylor gave Gabriella a look that said their conversation was far from over.

Gabriella rushed inside East High and began climbing the stairs that led to Troy's secret hideaway: a rooftop oasis of flowers and vegetables maintained by the Garden Club.

When Gabriella reached the top, she opened the door to the roof and found Troy standing near a trellis, which had three tuxedos hanging from it.

"You've got to help me with this," he said, grinning. "Which one should I wear?" he asked.

She smiled. "Because . . . ?" she asked.

"You're going to have a beautiful dress, and I want to look right," he explained.

Gabriella's face glowed. "I've never been asked to a prom, but this almost sounds like an invitation."

Troy reached into one of the tuxedo jackets and pulled out two tickets with the words EAST HIGH SENIOR PROM—LAST WALTZ printed on them.

Gabriella looked over at the tickets and smiled. She took a tuxedo jacket from the rack and helped him put it on over his T-shirt.

"Will we have to waltz?" Troy asked lightly, trying to cover up how nervous he felt. "I really don't know how to do that."

"All I know is what my dad showed me when I was a little girl," Gabriella said wistfully. "I'd stand on his toes, and he'd waltz me around the living room."

She looked over at Troy and gave him a shy glance. "Come here," she said.

They began dancing, awkwardly at first, as they tried to teach each other the steps. Soon, however, they were moving gracefully around the roof, smiling and gazing into each other's eyes. A light rain began to fall, but that didn't stop them. Waltzing, as it turned out, was too much fun.

Finally, they took a break.

"Is that a yes?" Troy asked.

"Yes," Gabriella replied.

As they happily looked at each other, the bell suddenly rang, forcing them to dash for the stairwell. Talking about the prom would have to wait until later.

Troy was still in a good mood later that afternoon when he headed for the gym. He spotted Jimmie and Donny stepping out of the shower area, wrapped in towels but still dripping wet. He grinned as he watched them reach their lockers and suddenly realize they were mysteriously open. *And* empty.

Troy paused for a few seconds to enjoy their confused expressions, then called out, "Yo, Rocketman . . ."

The two sophomores whirled around to see Troy and Chad leaning against a locker partition, holding Jimmie's and Donny's clothes.

"You guys wanted our lockers?" Troy asked.

"Well, it's moving day!" Chad announced.

Jimmie brightened immediately. "Sweet!"

Troy and Chad began walking toward the area where the varsity team's lockers were, closely followed by Jimmie and Donny. Troy counted the steps in his head—five, six, seven—then glanced over at Chad.

Suddenly, they both took off running, still carrying Jimmie's and Donny's things!

The two sophomores clutched their towels more tightly and gave chase through the Hall of Champions. When Donny saw that they were headed for the main hall, he yelled, "Hey, joke's over, guys!"

But Troy and Chad didn't stop. As students hooted and cheered, they raced through the hall, still pursued by Jimmie and Donny. The two boys were so intent on catching Troy and Chad they didn't even notice that they were being led toward the theater. Troy and Chad burst through a door, and Jimmie and Donny went flying right in after them—and suddenly found themselves onstage!

Center stage, in fact.

Holding their towels and still dripping wet.

The auditorium went silent as the students who were painting sets and studying scripts stopped what they were doing to gape at the scene. Kelsi even stopped playing the piano.

"Yearbook opportunity," Gabriella murmured to Taylor.

Taylor had already had the same thought. She nodded to the yearbook photographer who snapped a quick photo. "Got it!"

Ms. Darbus, who was used to improvisation and theatrical mishaps, took the situation in stride. "Bold choice, gentlemen, bold choice," she commented. "We must *all* have the courage to discover ourselves. However, at East High, we'll discover ourselves while clothed. But welcome to our spring musical," she said dryly. "And on with the show," she added.

★ ☆ ★

Later that afternoon, Troy and Gabriella pulled up in front of Gabriella's house in his truck. It came to a lurching stop.

"If my truck falls apart because I'm spending my free time onstage, it's all on you," Troy said, pretending to complain.

"*Me?*" Gabriella protested playfully.

"You think I'd be up there if it wasn't for you?" he joked.

She smiled at him for a moment before she answered, "Yeah, I do."

They hopped out of the truck and entered Gabriella's backyard. She turned and gave Troy a serious look.

"Troy, I watch you in rehearsal," she said. "You love it. Why is that so hard for you to admit?"

Troy looked sheepish. It was still difficult for him to believe how much he had changed since he had met Gabriella. A year ago, he didn't even know where the theater *was*, and he had never hung out with kids from the Drama Club—let alone tried out for a musical. But now . . . she was right. He did love it. Was it hard to admit that? Well . . .

"It isn't to you," he said. "But to my dad? To Chad? Yeah, that's a little hard."

"It shouldn't be," Gabriella told him.

Troy took a deep breath. It felt great being able to talk about everything he'd been feeling lately . . . especially with Gabriella. "They're happy as long as we're all talking about U of A. *You* chose Stanford . . . U of A was sort of chosen *for* me," he revealed. "I haven't been talking about this with anyone . . . but I've had offers from other colleges. And I'm really listening."

Gabriella looked at Troy sympathetically. "I get it, Troy. I've still got decisions to make, too."

"Like what?" Troy asked, surprised.

She opened her mouth to speak, but her mother chose that very moment to walk out onto Gabriella's balcony.

"I've got snacks for you inside . . ." she began. Mrs. Montez looked down at her daughter and Troy and noticed their serious expressions. "I think I interrupted something," she said slowly.

"Just talking, Mom," Gabriella replied quietly.

After all, there would be plenty of time to talk to Troy about everything later, she thought.

# CHAPTER 4

The next morning, Gabriella and Taylor met to work on the East High yearbook. On the computer, they clicked through action shots from the Wildcats' championship game and laid out pages as other yearbook staffers worked at their own desks.

A little while later, they were interrupted by Troy and Chad, who arrived with brownies. Gabriella reached out to grab one and said teasingly, "Kissing up to the yearbook editors. *Very* smart move."

"Chad's hoping for two pages for himself," Troy joked. "Maybe even a third page, just for his hair."

"Hey, what's right is right," Chad said, grinning. He looked at Troy as if suddenly struck by a thought. "Hoops, by the way, you've got to take me after school to check out the whole tuxedo thing."

Troy and Gabriella exchanged glances. "I'm definitely an expert," he said, smiling.

"Tuxedo?" Taylor asked. "What for?"

"Um . . . prom?" Chad answered.

Every other girl in the room turned to look at Chad with hopeful looks in their eyes.

Taylor, however, just lifted one mocking eyebrow and met Chad's gaze with a direct one of her own. "Honey, if that's what you call a formal invitation, you'll be dancing with yourself," she said haughtily.

She poked the basketball he was carrying under his arm, and it went rolling out into the hallway.

Meanwhile, Zeke and Jason were walking toward Sharpay's backstage dressing room. Zeke was a bundle of nerves, but Jason prodded him along and nudged him up the stairs.

Inside Sharpay's dressing room, Tiara was going through a box of photos. Tiara held up one

314

picture at a time for Sharpay's approval, dropping the yeses into a box for the yearbook staff and the nos into a box labeled EAST HIGH ARCHIVES.

"Yes," Sharpay said in response to a photo. "No . . . No . . . Yes . . . No . . ." She paused, then asked, "How many have I approved?"

Tiara knew the number without even checking. "Sixty-seven," she said confidently.

"That'll do," Sharpay said crisply. "Deliver those to the yearbook room."

Suddenly, a very nervous Zeke appeared in the doorway.

"Um . . . Sharpay . . . there's something I've been wanting to ask you for about a year . . ." he began haltingly. Even to his own ears, he sounded totally nervous. Fortunately, that didn't matter—because Sharpay wasn't even listening.

"Oh, Zeke, glad you stopped by," she said breezily. "You're taking me to prom. Don't buy a corsage, it's being flown in from Hawaii."

"I've sent the florist a fabric swatch," Tiara told Sharpay, her voice brisk and efficient.

Sharpay nodded, pleased, and went on, "Daddy will arrange limousine and restaurant."

Tiara stepped forward and began measuring Zeke's shoulders and arms.

"Your tuxedo will be delivered, but don't wear it to your ballroom-dance lessons," Sharpay added.

"Dance lessons?" Zeke asked. He looked dazed.

"Beginning Monday," Sharpay said. "Questions? No? Good. Toodles!"

Before he knew it, Zeke was headed back down the stairs, still shocked by his encounter with Sharpay. Jason was waiting for him at the foot of the stairs, wearing a T-shirt with the words JASON + MARTHA = PROM printed on the front.

Jason eyed Zeke closely. He really hoped that Zeke's mission to ask Sharpay had succeeded. Maybe, he thought, it will be a good omen for when I approach Martha . . .

"Well?" Jason asked eagerly.

Zeke gave him a weak smile. "I didn't even give her a chance to say no."

Troy saw Chad enter the cafeteria, a preoccupied look on his face. Before approaching him, Troy glanced around the room. At every table, clusters of students caught his eye and then quickly looked away.

Troy grinned. Perfect! Everything had been set up; now he just needed to put the plan into action.

He caught up with Chad and nudged him with his elbow, then pointed at the table where Taylor was sitting with Gabriella, Kelsi, and Martha.

"Now or never, dude," Troy said.

Chad looked nervous, but determined. "Okay, okay," he said. "I'm going in."

Troy reached into his backpack and pulled out a bunch of flowers cut from the rooftop garden. In one smooth motion, he took the basketball out of Chad's hand and replaced it with the bouquet. "The Garden Club is rooting for you," he told Chad.

Chad did not seem very reassured by the news, but he nodded and walked toward Taylor's table.

Without even saying hello, he blurted out, "So, anyway, I was really hoping you'd kind of go to the prom with me."

Troy bit his lip to keep from laughing. Smooth, Chad, he thought. *Real* smooth.

However, it seemed that Taylor hadn't even heard his clumsy attempt at an invitation. Or else she was pretending that she didn't hear. She glanced up at Chad and said, "Oh, hi, Chad. Hey, they've got Tuna Surprise on the menu. Your favorite."

"The prom," Chad said a little more louder. "I'm asking you."

Taylor shook her head, frowning slightly. "It's so loud in here," she said. "You'll have to speak up."

This was it! Troy raised his arm and the entire cafeteria fell silent just as Chad dropped to one knee and shouted, "Taylor McKessie, will you *please* be my date to the senior prom?"

For a long moment, Taylor just looked at him. Then she looked at her friends. Then she looked back at Chad.

"I'd be honored," she announced.

At that moment, the cafeteria burst into applause and cheers.

Troy patted Chad on the back and handed him his basketball.

"Dude, I need to go shoot some hoops," Chad said, who was very relieved his ordeal was over. "Right away," he added.

Fifteen minutes later, they were still dressed in their street clothes finishing a game of H-O-R-S-E in the gym. Troy took his turn and made a basket with ease. "Horse!" he called out.

"Go again?" Chad asked.

Troy shook his head. He knew what Chad was avoiding. As his best friend, Troy couldn't let him do it. "Dude, we can shoot hoops all day, but we still got to get you into a tuxedo," he said. "No way out, man."

A little while later, back in the theater, Ms. Darbus was commenting on the Wildcats' rehearsal. "Kelsi, the music is splendid, Ryan, your choreography is most inventive," Ms. Darbus began. She looked over at Jason and scowled. "Jason, we don't chew gum in the theater. . . ."

Chastened, Jason took the gum out of his mouth and put it in his shirt pocket.

Sharpay grabbed Ryan's arm and nodded

toward Kelsi. "I heard she's writing something amazing for Troy and Gabriella."

"A song, most likely," Ryan said mildly.

Sharpay's grip tightened. "Find out what it is!" she hissed.

She nudged Ryan toward the piano. He stumbled right in front of Kelsi, who was gathering her sheet music.

"So, hey, how can we make this whole show better?" he asked, fumbling for words as Sharpay glared at him. "Maybe we could get together?"

"I'm in the music room every morning as soon as they unlock the school," Kelsi said. "Actually, I have my own key, but don't tell anyone," she said shyly. "It's really early but . . . I do have a teapot. Come on by!"

Ryan smiled. That was pretty easy, he thought. Even if Sharpay had—literally—pushed him into it.

On the other side of the stage, Jimmie suddenly popped up in front of Troy. Troy jumped in surprise. Jimmie always seemed to startle him.

"Hey, good job, Troy!" Jimmie exclaimed.

"Stop doing that!" Troy told him, a little annoyed

320

that Jimmie had caught him off guard. *Again*. He glanced around the theater, wondering if there was some way he could slip away. Once Jimmie started talking, he never seemed to want to stop.

"Look, there's Sharpay!" Troy exclaimed. "You didn't hear this from me, but she has a secret crush on you," he then whispered to Jimmie.

Jimmie's face lit up. He swiveled around to look at Sharpay. Troy saw his chance to escape, and he took it.

As Jimmie headed in Sharpay's direction, Ms. Darbus grabbed him. "Mr. Zara?" she asked.

"Call me Rocketman if you want to," Jimmie answered.

"How generous," Ms. Darbus replied sarcastically. "And since you've been such a . . . dedicated presence here, I'm making you an understudy." She nodded toward Tiara, who had been hanging out at rehearsal every day, too. She had been running errands for Sharpay, bringing her cups of tea, and acting like the most efficient personal assistant in the world. Perhaps it was time, Ms. Darbus thought, to redirect that energy a bit. Say, toward the last production of the season. "Tiara, you as well."

"I'm in!" Jimmie pumped his fist in triumph and called out to his friend Donny, who was standing nearby. "Hey, Donny, I'm IN!!! I'm playing understudy."

Donny looked impressed. "Way cool. You rock, Jimmie Z!"

Tiara rolled her eyes. "Understudy isn't a role, you morons," she whispered. "It means you go on if one of the leads can't make it for the performance."

"Oh." Jimmie's face fell. "Well, you're one, too."

Tiara tossed her head. "The difference being, *I* can actually carry a tune."

"Hey, I wouldn't sing with you if my hair was on fire and you were the last bucket of water on Earth," Jimmie replied.

"And I wouldn't sing with you if I were starving and you were the last pickle at the picnic," Tiara said huffily.

They eyed each other for a long, interested moment.

"Want to have lunch sometime?" Jimmie asked.

Tiara smiled briefly and then walked away. She had already learned from Sharpay that it's always best to make a dramatic exit.

Later that day, Gabriella and Taylor were back in the yearbook room, working on their layouts. Gabriella seemed uncharacteristically subdued. Finally, she reached into her backpack and handed a letter to Taylor.

Taylor began to read the letter aloud. "Stanford University's freshman honors program cordially . . ." She stopped reading and reached out to give Gabriella a hug.

"Just tell me you've already said yes . . . right?" Taylor asked.

Gabriella shook her head. "I haven't even told my mom I got the letter."

Taylor gave Gabriella her patented "Taylor look." The one that meant "I can't *believe* you just said that!"

Gabriella was about to respond, but instinct made her glance at the door instead. She saw

Tiara standing there, holding the box of Sharpay's "approved" photos and smiling innocently.

Gabriella bit her lip. Tiara had obviously been standing there for a while. How much had she overheard?

Tiara stared intently at the monitor at one of the library's computer workstations. As she surfed the Internet, Sharpay leaned over her shoulder and peered closely at the screen.

At first, there were images of Stanford University. A few clicks later, and a photo of Gabriella, along with several other students, appeared. The headline on the page announced: STANFORD UNIVERSITY FRESHMAN HONOREES.

Tiara looked impressed. "They select only thirty freshmen from the entire incoming class," she explained to Sharpay. "It's a special three-week honors program."

"How prestigious," Sharpay quipped sarcastically.

Tiara scrolled down to read more. "But the program starts in two weeks!" she exclaimed. "She'd miss our"—she caught herself—"*your* show."

"Oh, my goodness!" Sharpay said in mock despair. "What to do?"

Sharpay smiled smugly as the beginning of a scheme began to form in her mind. "Well, the show must go on . . . mustn't it?"

## CHAPTER 5

Ryan arrived at East High very early the next morning. He looked around the courtyard. It was eerily empty at this hour, with no crowds of students, no laughing, no jostling, no yelling . . .

In fact, he thought, it was a rather nice change.

He went inside and made his way to the music room. As he slipped inside, he noticed the morning light streaming through the windows, casting a glow around the grand piano, kettle drums, music stands . . . and Kelsi, who was perched on top of a piano and looking out the window, lost in thought.

He sat down quietly at the grand piano. The

music sheet in front of him read, "Just Want to Be with You," Kelsi Nielsen . . . duet Troy/Gabriella." He began picking out part of the melody on the piano. Kelsi turned around, and he smiled at her.

"Kind of beautiful," he said, giving her a shy smile.

She shrugged, but she looked pleased. "Stuck on the bridge," she admitted. "Worried about the show . . ."

"Shouldn't be," he said. "It's sounding good. The prom number was great. So is this one."

He continued playing for a moment. Then he looked at her and asked, "So . . . what are you doing prom night?"

"It's two days before the show," she replied. "I'll be working on charts and fixing orchestrations and probably changing song lyrics right up until—"

"Good," Ryan interrupted. "Pick you up at eight."

It took Kelsi a moment to understand what Ryan had just said—but when she did, she gave him a big smile. Then she sat on the piano bench beside him, and they finished playing the song as a duet.

★ ☆ ★

**A** few hours later, Kelsi was still playing the same song, but now she was in the theater's orchestra pit with the rhythm section. Other students were also there rehearsing. The set was a house with a balcony—one that looked remarkably like the balcony at Gabriella's house—and a large tree that "grew" right out of the orchestra pit. Gabriella was sitting on the balcony, and Troy was climbing the tree to reach her as Ryan, Sharpay, and Ms. Darbus watched.

Troy and Gabriella sang the song Kelsi wrote for them with great emotion. As the last notes of "Just Want to Be with You" drifted away, Ryan told them, "Pity the actor who has to follow that in the show." He stopped, struck by a dismaying thought. "Wait. It might be me."

Gabriella smiled warmly at him. "The way you dance, you've got no worries."

"Yeah, we're all trying to catch up with you," Troy added.

Ryan felt a glow of happiness—not just because of the compliments, but because he really loved being around his friends. Last year, he would never have imagined in his wildest dreams that a brainiac like Gabriella or a jock like Troy would be his friends. But now . . .

"Ryan?" Sharpay's voice sliced through his thoughts.

Sighing, he walked over to where his sister was standing in the wings.

"Did you get a copy of that song from Kelsi?" she asked.

"No, but I'm taking her to the prom!" Ryan exclaimed.

"Brilliant!" Sharpay looked more pleased with this news than he would have expected. He understood why when she added, "Keep your friends close and your enemies closer. Now, get me that duet."

"Um . . ." Ryan hesitated, a little scared to say what he was thinking. Then he took a deep breath and said bravely, "Last time I checked, you're not Gabriella."

To his surprise, Sharpay didn't yell at him for this tiny insubordination. She didn't scream. She didn't even frown. Instead, she looked smug.

"Don't be so sure," she told Ryan, as she turned to walk backstage.

Later that afternoon, Taylor was at Gabriella's house. They had yearbook materials spread out all over Gabriella's bedroom, and Gabriella was doing her best to concentrate on the work they had to do. But Taylor couldn't focus. They had something they needed to talk about, and she wasn't going to let the yearbook get in the way.

"You should be throwing a party, not keeping a secret," Taylor told her firmly.

"But it starts at Stanford next week!" Gabriella cried. They had gone over this a hundred times. Why couldn't Taylor understand? She tried one more time to make her position clear. "I'll miss everything!"

"You'll come back for prom and graduation," Taylor countered. "You had enough credits to graduate from East High last December. Sister, your future is calling, loud and clear."

Gabriella sighed with frustration. "Stop being my mom for a second and just be my friend!" she protested. "Maybe I like it here. Maybe I want to stay in Albuquerque as long as possible."

She paused and then decided to finally open up and say the thing she had barely let herself think about, the thing that she knew would shock Taylor more than anything else. "Maybe I'll just stay *here* next year."

Sure enough, Taylor's eyes opened wide. "WHAT?!!!"

While Gabriella and Taylor were having a heart-to-heart, Troy and Chad were bouncing down a back road in Troy's beat-up truck. They finally came to a halt at a junkyard filled with rusted old cars and trucks in various stages of disrepair. A basketball hoop was nailed up on the fence, and the rough markings of a basketball court were outlined in the dirt.

Mr. Riley, the junkyard's owner, sauntered over to the truck.

"My fuel pump is deceased, Mr. Riley," Troy said ruefully.

Mr. Riley grinned. "Dig around, you'll find one

here. Can't wait to see you guys play for U of A next year. Already bought my season tickets." He tossed Chad the keys to the gate. "Lock up when you leave."

Troy and Chad opened the gate and walked over to a giant pile of spare parts. They began searching for a fuel pump.

"Hear that?" Chad asked. "Season tickets. Time to start practicing, dude."

"Take a breather, LeBron," Troy said as he dug through the pile. "Man, don't you ever feel like your entire life is already being laid out for you?"

Chad gave him a puzzled look. "What's your point?"

"I just want my future to be . . . *my* future," Troy said.

"See what happens when you do a show?" Chad asked jokingly. "You're like . . . five people."

Troy bristled a bit, even though he knew Chad was just teasing. "What's so bad about that?" he asked. "When we used to come here as kids, we'd be ten people! Spies, superheroes, rock stars . . . we were whatever we wanted to be, whenever we wanted to be it. It was us, man!"

"We were eight years old," Chad pointed out. Then he grinned. "And for the record, I was a much better superhero than you."

He snatched up a piece of metal and brandished it like a sword. Troy laughed and grabbed a piece of his own. Suddenly, they were both acting like kids, jumping from car to car, sword fighting among the piles of rusty parts. They were laughing so hard they were doubled over. It was almost as if they were replaying every moment from their years of friendship. And they were having a blast doing it.

Finally, they stopped and tried to catch their breath. They stood next to each other in the approaching dusk, still panting.

Gradually, boyhood slipped away once more, and the future loomed on the horizon again, both tantalizing and terrifying.

"What are you going to do if Juilliard says yes?" Chad asked.

"I don't know," Troy admitted.

Chad's high spirits fell a bit. "That's not what I wanted to hear," he said. "I'm getting you back in the gym tomorrow."

He shoved Troy playfully, and they piled into the truck, ready to go home.

**B**ack at Gabriella's house, Taylor was shocked at what Gabriella had just told her.

"Stay in Albuquerque?" Taylor gasped. "That makes no sense."

She was sitting on the bed in Gabriella's room, trying to recover from what her friend had just said.

"And why do I always have to make sense?" Gabriella argued. "I'll still go to Stanford. But maybe in a year. I can take classes at U of A. I don't know."

"U of A?" Taylor couldn't believe what she was hearing. "You're not thinking clearly, because you're thinking about Troy. He's your first crush. But there'll be more boys, more Troys."

Gabriella turned around and spotted her mother standing in the doorway. Great! First she had Taylor on her case. Now she was going to have to explain herself to her mother.

Gabriella couldn't deal with that right then. She ran out onto the balcony to be by herself.

Mrs. Montez and Taylor exchanged identical, and worried, glances.

They both wanted what was best for Gabriella— but would she be able to see that?

Later that evening, the Bolton and Danforth families were having a celebration dinner at Troy's house. Chad was proudly wearing his new U of A jersey. Troy was trying to put up a good front, but he really wasn't feeling that festive.

"First U of A game is at home against Trinity," Troy's dad said. "But the next game is away . . . against Tulane."

"That's New Orleans, right?" Mrs. Bolton asked.

"Road trip!" Mr. Danforth exclaimed. He gave Troy's dad a high five.

Troy smiled weakly. He wished he could be as excited as everyone else was. But he was just so confused. He knew he had to make a decision about college. And soon.

Gabriella was still on her balcony, looking up at the starry night sky, when her mother opened the door and stepped out.

Her mother looked at Gabriella with concern. "High school feels like the most important thing in the world. When you're in it. But that changes," she said gently.

"Not everything has to change, Mom," Gabriella said. "I don't believe that."

Mrs. Montez knew what Gabriella was feeling. She also knew enough to stop talking. She just gave her daughter a quick hug and went back inside.

Dinner was finished at the Bolton house. The Danforths had gone home, and Troy's parents were clearing the kitchen. Troy was out in the backyard, shooting hoops. He stopped for a moment to watch his parents through the window. It was a familiar scene. His mom and dad smiled and talked softly to each other as they put the dishes away, the same way they had for as long as he could remember.

He looked away from them. That was becoming a part of his past now. Pretty soon, he wouldn't be living here, wouldn't be having dinner at home almost every night, and wouldn't be watching his parents do the same things that he had long ago started taking for granted.

He put his basketball on the ground and headed toward his treehouse. He climbed up the stairs and then stared up at the sky. The stars looked even more distant and unreachable than usual—as distant and unreachable as his own future. Without quite realizing it, he began to sing a few bars of "Right Here, Right Now," another song that Kelsi wrote for the musical, the tempo slow and meditative. . . .

A few miles away, Gabriella was by herself on her balcony, singing the same song. Despite all the confusion she was feeling, singing made her feel calm—almost as if Troy were sitting beside her and singing, too.

Together, Troy and Gabriella sang a duet without even knowing it.

Or, maybe, in some way, they did.

# CHAPTER 6

The next morning, Gabriella was standing at her locker, organizing her books for the day, when Troy slid around the corner. He pulled out his cell phone and began scrolling through photos of flowers.

"Okay, prom corsages," he said, holding out the phone so Gabriella could see a picture of each flower as it came up on the screen. "Take your pick, because if you leave it up to me . . . well . . ."

"If you pick it out, I'm going to like it," Gabriella said. She took another look at the corsages and added with a laugh, "Unless it's that one."

Suddenly, the bell rang. They smiled at each other and headed off to their separate classes.

Later that day, Troy was at his locker gathering his books. He closed the locker door and was startled to see Sharpay standing there.

"Hi, Troy!" Sharpay said brightly. "I realized I haven't offered my congratulations."

"Thanks, but to tell you the truth, I'm glad the season's over," Troy replied politely.

"I didn't mean basketball, silly," she said with a mischievous grin. "I meant Gabriella."

"Huh?" Troy asked.

Sharpay gave Troy a serious look. "Her missing the show is a little disappointing. But being selected for Stanford's freshman honors program . . . well, that's amazing for her."

Troy looked at her in confusion. "I don't know what you're talking about," he said.

"Everyone else does," Sharpay said matter-of-factly. "The whole school is buzzing. The honorees get to spend time with Stanford's top professors in special classes. Starting next week."

"Next week?" Troy asked in surprise.

339

Sharpay looked at him pitifully. "You *really* didn't know?" she asked. "Okay, this is a little awkward. I guess her not telling you means she's on the fence about it. But who better than Troy Bolton to encourage her to accept that honor, since the only thing possibly holding her back is . . . you."

With that, Sharpay walked off, leaving a dumbfounded Troy standing at his locker.

That night, Gabriella was doing homework in her room when her cell phone rang. She answered distractedly and heard a strange voice say, "Pizza's here."

She frowned. "I didn't order pizza," she told the caller.

Then she heard Troy, using his regular voice, say, "You didn't have to."

Smiling, she stepped out onto the balcony and into the warm night air. She turned to see him standing in the backyard, holding a pizza box.

He looked at Gabriella and grinned. "Half vegetarian, half everything else. Oh, and let's not forget—"

He put the box down and grabbed the rope that was hanging over the balcony. He pulled up a box that was rigged to the rope and added, "What's a picnic without chocolate-covered strawberries?"

Gabriella shook her head, giggling. "You are one crazy Wildcat."

Troy climbed up the tree near Gabriella's balcony, while Gabriella hoisted up the basket from the ground and then began laying out their food. Fifteen minutes later, they had worked their way through half the pizza, and Troy had managed to gather the courage to bring up the subject he had come to talk about.

"So," he said nervously, "here's the thing. Your freshman honors program at Stanford . . ."

"How'd you hear about that?" Gabriella interrupted.

"A lot of people heard about it," Troy said quietly. "But I wasn't one of them. Why?"

"Because I knew what you would say!" she exclaimed defensively.

"Of course you should do the honors program," he told her. He couldn't believe that she would actually consider *not* going.

341

Gabriella looked down. "I've been thinking about trying to talk my mom into letting me stay in Albuquerque another year. Take some classes here, go to Stanford when I'm ready," she admitted.

Troy looked at her in shock. "You can't just put off something as amazing as Stanford!" he cried.

Gabriella sighed with exasperation. "So maybe I get to be a little crazy," she admitted. "Everything about my life has been full-speed ahead. This is the first time I've ever even wanted it all to slow down . . . to a stop."

"We're going to graduate," he pointed out. "That's going to happen." Whether we want to or not, he thought.

"Does everything feel that easy for you?" Gabriella asked. "Lucky you, I guess. I get it, it's senior year. This is what happens. But you know what, Troy, my heart doesn't know it's in high school."

*That* stopped him. He gave her a searching look. Troy started to say something, but Gabriella interrupted him. "Don't say anything else. I'm way better at good-byes than you." She smiled faintly. "I've had a lot of practice."

She kissed him on the cheek and stood up to go inside.

"Wait," Troy said. One word had jumped out at him. "Why are you saying 'good-bye'? You'll be back for prom and graduation."

She hesitated, then said, "I meant good night."

Back inside her bedroom, Gabriella finally let the tears fall. She knew it was right to attend the honors program and prepare to leave East High behind—but she couldn't help thinking of all the fun she had had and the friends she had made since arriving in Albuquerque.

And Troy . . .

Moments of their time flashed through her mind. Their first meeting at the New Year's Eve party, doing karaoke and finding an unknown side of themselves . . . performing in *Twinkle Towne* . . . working together over the summer at the country club . . . having fun with their friends in the talent show . . .

Gradually, the memories seemed to fade and drift away. That was the past.

She sighed and began to pack some boxes. Like it or not, she was headed into the future.

As soon as Gabriella left for Stanford, East High seemed to become a totally different place.

Troy knew she had made the right decision, but that didn't help when he sat in the rooftop garden . . . alone.

Gabriella's friends were proud of her, but they still missed her when they ate lunch in the cafeteria and noticed her empty seat. Even homeroom wasn't the same without Gabriella.

But perhaps her absence was felt most in the theater. Rehearsals for the spring musical continued, of course, but Troy's heart wasn't really in it. Neither was Kelsi's. Or Taylor's. Or Chad's.

Ms. Darbus could tell that some of the students were dismayed, but they still had a production to rehearse.

"With Miss Montez unavailable to us, the show must go on," Ms. Darbus said firmly. "Sharpay, you'll do Gabriella's duet with Troy. Tiara, are you ready to step in for Sharpay?"

Tiara beamed but tried to look modest. "Those shoes are impossible to fill, Ms. Darbus."

Sharpay gave Tiara a gracious nod of appreciation. "Kelsi will work with you," she told Tiara. "All right, let's get going. Where's Troy?"

Everyone looked around.

But Troy was nowhere to be found.

In fact, Troy was nowhere in the building. He was home, missing Gabriella. He went into the kitchen for a snack and heard a basketball bouncing in the backyard. He headed outside and found his dad shooting hoops.

His dad tossed him the ball. Troy caught it and then sunk a basket.

"How's the big show going?" his father asked, catching the ball as it bounced on the concrete.

Troy sighed. "You don't want to know."

His dad spun around and tried for a basket. He missed. Troy grabbed the rebound and started maneuvering for his own shot.

"If I'm honest, I'm glad you're getting tired of it," his dad admitted. "I mean, when did you plan to tell me about this Juilliard thing?"

"Nothing to tell," Troy said, trying to sound casual, just before he launched the ball in the air.

This time he missed the shot. His dad caught the ball and stood still.

"Well, maybe there is," he said slowly. "I'm hearing you're thinking about other schools."

Troy glanced at his dad uncomfortably. "U of A isn't the only school that's talked to me, Dad. You know that."

"But it's the only school *we've* talked about," Mr. Bolton said. "Hey, Chad would be pretty disappointed if you changed your mind, for one thing."

"He'd get over it," Troy replied. "Would you?" he asked.

His dad sighed. "We've been going to U of A games ever since you were a little kid. All you ever talked about is being in a Redhawk uniform."

Troy nodded, but he had to finally be honest with his father. "Only thing is, I'm not a little kid anymore. You raised me to make my own choices. I'm the one who needs to make them, not you or Chad or anyone else."

Troy turned and headed toward the house.

"Hey, Troy . . ." his dad called out.

But Troy didn't turn around. Coach Bolton walked inside, just in time to see Troy heading out the front door and getting into his truck. Coach Bolton started to follow, but his wife reached out a hand to stop him, an understanding expression on her face.

Troy was trying to figure out where he was going next—and his parents were trying to figure out how to let him go.

Troy knew exactly what would make him feel more at ease. He headed to East High and used his "secret key" to open the door to the Wildcats' locker room. He glanced over at his locker and continued walking down the Hall of Champions. He headed toward the theater and got up on the stage, the place where he and Gabriella had learned something important about themselves and each other. He thought about what next year would be like, without his friends, his team, and Gabriella, and suddenly he felt like screaming.

Instead, he sang a song he'd been learning for the musical, a song that expressed all the confusion and heartache he was feeling.

From the darkness came the sound of one person clapping.

Troy looked up, startled to see Ms. Darbus coming down the aisle.

"Um . . . I know I'm not supposed to be here, Ms. Darbus . . ." he began.

The drama teacher looked at him curiously. "Nor am I, but I'm trying to rebalance a show in which Sharpay is now playing Miss Montez." She gave him a shrewd, questioning look. "And the reason for your visit is . . . ?"

He hesitated. "I guess I feel like this is a really good place to—" He stopped, embarrassed.

"Scream?" she suggested. "Feel free."

"Or just to think," he said.

She nodded. "The stage is a wonderful partner in the process of self-discovery," she said. "You seem very comfortable up there."

"I do?" Troy asked, surprised.

"Yes," she replied with conviction. "Which is why I submitted an application in your name to Juilliard."

"It was you?" he asked, sounding even more surprised.

"Better to consider these opportunities now, than in ten years when life might limit your choices," she said, her voice softening a bit. "If I've overstepped, I apologize."

He shook his head. "I'm not mad . . . just confused."

"What I've learned from the stage is to trust one's instincts," she said. "And that takes courage, a quality you don't seem to lack." As she walked away, she added, "Stay as long as you like. Last one out turns off the lights."

# CHAPTER 7

**G**radually, Gabriella got used to being at Stanford. At first it was a little scary—all those new people, new professors, and a dorm room. But it was also really cool. As she walked to her first class, she spotted a sign that said WELCOME FRESHMAN HONORS CLASS—and it was printed in five languages! She grinned and felt a small thrill of excitement. It *was* amazing to be here, at the university she had dreamed about attending for so many years, and to be meeting people from all over the world.

Still, she couldn't help but wonder what her old friends were doing back at East High. . . .

The East High auditorium was buzzing with activity, just as it had before every other big show. Unfortunately, not all of the activity was going particularly well.

In fact, almost none of it was.

Troy and Chad were snapping at each other. Sharpay was bossing Ryan around even more than usual. And Zeke and Jason just goofed off the entire time, until finally they actually knocked down an entire set!

The musical was falling apart in front of everyone's eyes. And no one was more dismayed than Kelsi, who was watching the disaster unfold with an impending sense of doom. She sat slumped on her piano bench, her head in her hands, when Troy approached her.

"Hey, I'm sorry I've been messing up your songs a little," he said.

She brushed his apology aside. "It's all of us!" she cried. "And all of us pretty much know why. If it wasn't for Gabriella, our last musical would just be the Sharpay show."

He nodded as he thought that over. He knew exactly what she meant.

That same day, Gabriella was standing in the university quad near a fountain, taking in the college scene around her.

She saw students rushing to class, lying on the grass reading and exchanging hellos.

She saw friends walking together, talking and laughing.

She saw couples walking hand in hand.

She took it all in, deep in thoughts of her own.

A few days later, Troy and Chad walked into the Boltons' kitchen after picking up Troy's tuxedo at the rental shop. Troy showed it to his mom, who looked impressed.

"Wow, gorgeous!" she exclaimed.

"I'd like to take credit, but Gabriella picked it out," Troy said.

"And I've ordered a corsage that's going to perfectly match her dress," his mom said with a smile.

Just then, Troy's cell phone rang. He looked at his phone and saw Gabriella's picture. He smiled. It's almost like we have ESP, he thought as he answered.

When he listened to what Gabriella had to say, however, his smile gradually disappeared. "Don't even say that!" he argued, trying to stop what he was hearing. He headed toward his bedroom.

"Gabriella, the prom is in two days," he protested. "You're supposed to be on an airplane."

She sighed. "It's taken me two weeks to get used to being away from you, from East High, and from all my friends," she said, doing her best to make him understand.

Chad was worried as he stood in the hallway and listened to Troy's conversation. He didn't need to hear what Gabriella was saying to know this phone call wasn't going well.

But Troy wasn't aware of Chad standing there. He took a deep breath and continued to listen.

"So I come back and go to the prom and I leave again? And then it's graduation, and I leave again?" Gabriella's voice trembled. "I don't think I can do it. I think I've run out of good-byes, Troy.

I really have. I need to stay right where I am. I'm sorry."

She hung up the phone in tears.

Troy stared at the now silent phone, stunned. "She's not coming back," he said quietly.

"What?" Chad was shocked. "And miss prom?"

Troy nodded.

"Whoa," Chad replied. "Hey, that's lousy, man. It really is."

Chad could tell this wasn't helping much. He tried to think of something that would cheer up Troy, get his mind off his troubles . . .

And just like that, he knew exactly the right words to say. "School ends, and you don't take the girl with you, right? Gabriella is one step ahead, as usual." He gave Troy a meaningful look. "But now, you snap out of it, dude. We're all starting over. She's at Stanford, Taylor's heading to Yale. We're at U of A. Whole new ball game."

That should do it, Chad thought, satisfied. It was as good a pep talk as any he had ever given the Wildcats, and those had always worked.

Troy looked at Chad in frustration. "Maybe I don't see my life as a 'ball game' anymore, okay?"

The two friends stared at each other, each of them unsure about what to say next.

Troy thought about what Chad had just said. Maybe this time, he thought, he would be one step ahead of Gabriella. And then he knew exactly what he had to do.

# CHAPTER 8

Two days later, dusk was beginning to fall as the Wildcats started arriving at East High for the prom. The gym had been transformed with lights and decorations into a fantasyland. Chad and Taylor walked through the entrance, smiling and looking around in disbelief at the gym where so many hard-fought basketball games had been played. They were closely followed by Sharpay and Zeke, Ryan and Kelsi, and Martha and Jason. But two particular people were quite obviously missing. . . .

★ ☆ ★

$B$ack at Stanford, Gabriella was sitting alone in a classroom, finishing a very long equation on the chalkboard and trying to not think about the prom. She knew that it was about time for it to start. Her friends were probably arriving at the gym right now, dressed in their prom finery. Fortunately, she had this extremely complicated math problem to focus on, which helped to keep her thoughts off the dance and all the fun she was missing. . . .

And then she solved the equation.

She stood still for a moment, looking at the board. Sighing, she picked up her book bag and headed out into the golden late-afternoon sunlight.

This late in the day, the quad was almost deserted. As Gabriella walked toward her dorm, she glanced over at the parking area and did a double take. For a moment, she thought she spotted Troy's truck there. But how could that be, when Troy was back in Albuquerque? Maybe, she thought, she just missed him so much that she was seeing things. . . .

"Figured you'd be the last one out of the building," a voice said from behind her.

She whirled around. Now she was *sure* that she was hearing things because that voice sounded exactly like Troy's.

Something made her look up into the branches of a nearby tree—and there he was, wearing a tuxedo and basketball shoes. He grinned down at her.

"I don't believe this!" She gasped.

"I took a wrong turn on the way to my prom," he said. "And so did you."

She started to smile. "You're so crazy. What is it about you and trees?"

He shrugged. "I see things clearly from up here."

"You look handsome," she said, taking in his elegant attire. "But prom is . . . tonight. In Albuquerque. And that's a thousand miles away."

He shook his head. "My prom is wherever you are," he said in a serious tone. He tossed her a corsage. "And if I'm going to have a last dance at East High, it's going to be with you."

Gabriella hesitated slightly, then held out her hand. Troy jumped down from the tree and took her in his arms.

They began dancing around the quad, just as they had when they were learning to waltz together in the school's rooftop garden. Troy twirled Gabriella out, and when she twirled back, she felt as if she was actually wearing her prom dress. She gazed into Troy's eyes and smiled.

As they continued to dance around the quad under a giant tree at their own private prom, their friends were dancing, too. The other Wildcats swept across the gym floor in each other's arms and somehow, they all felt that Troy and Gabriella were there with them.

The sun was setting by the time Troy and Gabriella had finished dancing. They strolled around the quad, enjoying the last light of the day.

"It's the best prom I could have imagined, Troy," Gabriella said dreamily.

359

"Well, if I learned to waltz, it's all your fault," Troy joked.

He then looked at Gabriella seriously. "But it's not just me who changed when you came to East High," he continued. "Kids I used to just pass in the hallway, now we're all friends. And we're all supposed to do a show together. East High changed when you got there, and now it's changed because you left."

Troy took a step back and looked into Gabriella's eyes. "You may be ready to say good-bye to East High, but East High isn't ready to say good-bye to you."

# CHAPTER 9

The sign in front of the theater at East High read: TONIGHT—A HIGH SCHOOL MUSICAL—SENIOR YEAR.

A buzz of anticipation filled the auditorium as the audience members took their seats. But behind the scenes there was a different kind of buzz—the buzz of total chaos! The cast was warming up and trying to settle their nerves, the tech crew was making last-minute checks of the sound and lights, and the costume department was trying to make sure everyone's clothes looked just right.

Sharpay swept grandly through all of the confusion, heading for her dressing room. Suddenly, Jimmie popped out in front of her from behind a curtain.

"We haven't formally met, even though I feel we know each other on a . . . sort of vibey level," he said confidently. "I'm Jimmie 'the Rocket' Zara. And—"

"'Jimmie *the Rocket*'?" Sharpay asked in disbelief. "What are you, some sort of Muppet gangster?"

She suddenly caught a whiff of his cologne. And it did *not* smell good. She sneezed violently.

"Is that your cologne or a toxic spill?" she snipped.

"I bought it for the show," he explained eagerly. "It's called Babe Magnet."

Sharpay rolled her eyes. "Get out of my way!" she huffed. She turned to the stage manager. "Send Troy in to see me; we need to run the song."

She shoved Jimmie aside and stomped away just as his cell phone beeped.

He pulled it out of his pocket. His face lit up when he saw who was sending the text message.

"Hey, it's Troy," Jimmie said to Donny, who was standing next to him. And then, just to make sure Donny got the point—*Troy Bolton was contacting Jimmie!*—he added, "Troy Bolton is sending me a text. Checking in."

Then he read the text out loud. "'Been driving all night. I'll try and get there for the second act. Break a leg.'" He looked at Donny, puzzled. "'Break a leg?' I don't get it."

Donny grinned at him. "Dude, I think it's showbiz for 'you're going on.'"

Jimmie's face turned pale. "As *Troy*?" he asked, hoping that he had misunderstood. "On*stage*?"

"That *so* rocks!" Donny exclaimed. He sounded genuinely excited for his friend.

Of course Donny sounds psyched, Jimmie thought. *He* isn't the guy doomed to make a fool of himself in front of the cast and crew, and a packed auditorium! Jimmie would never live this down, *never*. And his high school career had been going *so well* up until now. . . .

Fortunately, Jimmie's bleak thoughts were interrupted by Ms. Darbus, who rushed up to them and asked, "No Troy?"

When they shook their heads, she said to Donny, "Get word to Kelsi." She turned to Jimmie, who looked as if he were frozen in place.

"Ms. Darbus, I think he stopped breathing!" Donny exclaimed.

She looked around for help. "Get him oxygen!" she yelled. "It's showtime!"

Kelsi was standing in the orchestra pit, ready to bring down her baton to start the overture. Just as the lights dimmed, Donny jumped into the pit and whispered something in her ear.

For just a second, her eyes widened with alarm. Then she took a deep breath. Whatever happened tonight, happened. This musical was about to begin, and nothing could stop it.

She brought down her baton. The music swelled and *Senior Year* began! A whistle blew loudly. Cheerleaders charged onto the stage to join Wildcats basketball players for the big "championship game" scene. Chad took center stage as the Wildcats won—again!

The audience's cheering was as enthusiastic as it had been at the actual championship game. Chad grinned and realized that being onstage performing in a musical wasn't so goofy after all. Without thinking, he turned to catch Troy's eye— and then he remembered. Troy wasn't there. A little deflated, Chad exited to the wings.

As the singing and dancing continued onstage, Sharpay was in her dressing room putting the finishing touches on her makeup. Once she was satisfied that her lip gloss was absolutely perfect, she hung out backstage to watch Ryan finish his big song, "I Want It All," surrounded by dancers doing high kicks.

He did a good job, Sharpay thought, as applause filled the room. Quite respectable, in fact. But now, *now* it was finally *her* chance! And she was going to show everyone how a *real* star performed!

She swept through the French doors that led to the balcony set. The audience clapped and cheered for her dramatic entrance. She began singing "Just Want to Be with You," and turned to where Troy should have been standing to join her in their duet.

But Troy was still nowhere to be found.

Sharpay looked around anxiously, a noticeable frown on her face.

Missing a cue during a live performance was an unpardonable mistake! Not *only* did it disrupt the play, but it made *her* look bad! She would certainly have something to say to Troy as soon as this scene was over!

Her angry thoughts were interrupted by a sudden noise behind her. Jimmie, dressed in a combination of Wildcats' basketball gear and fancy clothes, had stumbled onto the balcony. Sharpay whirled around.

Then Jimmie, his eyes wide with panic, started singing. And it was clear from the first note that he was not a good singer.

Sharpay was livid. Her mind raced as she tried to figure out how she could possibly save this scene, this play, and, in fact, her whole career—but before she could come up with a plan of action, there was another disaster.

She started sneezing.

And it wasn't just one little sneeze, the kind that could easily be covered up. It was a full-blown, serial sneeze attack!

The audience roared. Her eyes watering, Sharpay stalked off the stage, just in time to see Troy and Gabriella burst through the back door.

Troy was dressed in his jeans and tuxedo jacket; Gabriella was wearing her Stanford sweater. They headed straight for the stage, passing Sharpay, who was still sneezing and coughing and trying to make her way to her dressing room.

"Perfect," she snapped as they ran past her. *Of course* Troy and Gabriella were here to save the day—and steal her spotlight. Why shouldn't history repeat itself? "Go for it. Save the day. Whoopee," she said with defeat.

As she walked wearily to her dressing room, Troy and Gabriella ran toward the stage. Troy jumped down to the orchestra pit to climb the tree to the balcony where Gabriella would be waiting.

Their sudden appearance surprised everyone—and lifted everyone's spirits, too. Gabriella and

Troy began singing "Just Want to Be with You." The entire cast was smiling. Suddenly, the show was fantastic!

When Sharpay finally made it to her dressing room, she discovered Tiara sitting in front of her makeup mirror, wearing one of her dresses.

Sharpay's mouth dropped open. It took her several seconds to understand what she was seeing. Then she yelled, "That's my dress!"

Tiara nodded calmly. "Had one made just like it. Only better." She smiled at Sharpay in the mirror. "I'm playing Sharpay, remember? Do you mind stepping aside? I need to warm up and give a good first impression, since it will be *my* drama department next year."

Sharpay's mind was reeling. What was happening here? Where had the meek, unassuming, hero-worshipping Tiara gone? And who was this upstart in her place?

"You're not a singer, you're a London schoolgirl!" Sharpay protested.

Tiara smiled smugly. "Yes . . . London Academy

of Dramatic Arts. I took the job with you to learn the theater ropes at East High. Now I have."

"But you were so . . . humble!" Sharpay insisted.

"That's called acting," Tiara replied. "You should try it sometime."

Then she swept out of the room and onto the stage for her scene.

Tiara began to sing "A Night to Remember" in her role as Sharpay. Listening from the dressing room, Sharpay had to admit that Tiara sounded good. *Really* good.

Life was so terribly unfair.

She put her head down on the dressing table and sighed. She had been defeated, and she knew it. Sharpay could hear the audience cheering—not for her, but for the person who was playing her!

Life was *despicably* unfair.

Then, deep inside of Sharpay, her fighting instinct began to kick in.

She lifted her head. So what if life wasn't always picture-perfect? She was Sharpay Evans—and no little pip-squeak imitator could take that away from her!

She began shadowboxing in the mirror to psych herself up. Then she said to her reflection, "If East High is going to remember one Sharpay . . . it's going to be *me!*"

She noted with approval that her reflection looked determined, purposeful, and powerful. In other words, like the *real* Sharpay Evans. She ran to her clothes rack and began sifting through her wardrobe. She had to find the perfect outfit and she had to find it *now.*

Tiara was still onstage, still singing, still basking in the limelight—when suddenly the crowd gasped.

Sharpay was being lowered to the stage from the rafters, dressed in the same dress Tiara was wearing, only with more bling, more flounce, more star presence. She landed right in front of her new rival and began to sing.

And then East High was treated to a singing showdown that would be remembered for years to come! It was Sharpay versus Tiara, two superstar divas who both loved the spotlight—and neither would give an inch. As they sang a dueling version of "A Night to Remember," the rest of the cast and crew watched in awe.

It was a showstopper to end all showstoppers, and when it was over, the curtain fell. *Senior Year* was a smashing success.

# CHAPTER 10

The curtain rose again, revealing the cast wearing their caps and gowns.

"Ladies and gentlemen," Ms. Darbus announced, "our seniors."

As she read their names, each student took his or her turn in the spotlight.

"Martha Cox," Ms. Darbus said. "University of Southern California. Dance."

Martha bowed, grinning from ear to ear.

"Zeke Baylor," Ms. Darbus continued. "Teen Chef of the Year, Cornell University. Culinary."

He bowed with a flourish.

"Kelsi Nielsen. The Juilliard School. Music."

Kelsi froze in the spotlight before taking her bow, shock written all over her face. She couldn't believe she won the Juilliard scholarship.

"Jason Cross." As Jason moved into the spotlight, she added dryly, "You did it. You graduated."

Jason cast his eyes to the ceiling in thanks and then moved to the side.

"Taylor McKessie," Ms. Darbus called out. "Yale University. Magna Cum Laude. Political Science."

Taylor tried to play it cool, but she couldn't help showing how excited she was.

As Sharpay and Ryan stood next to each other, waiting their turn, Ms. Darbus glanced at the note in her hand.

"I'm pleased to announce that due to the excellence displayed here this evening, Juilliard has made an extraordinary decision," she said. "Another senior is now offered a Juilliard scholarship . . ."

As everyone in the audience seemed to turn their attention toward Sharpay, she broke out into a huge smile.

Ms. Darbus knew how to create drama. She

paused for just a moment before saying, "Congratulations, Mr. Ryan Evans. Choreography."

Stunned, Ryan glanced nervously at his sister. He didn't know how Sharpay was going to handle the news.

But Sharpay pushed him gently toward the center of the stage and then led the applause.

As Sharpay stood onstage, smiling at her brother, Ms. Darbus added, "And as I will be taking a sabbatical next fall, I can now reveal with great pride my choice to run East High's Drama Department during my absence." She turned and gestured to Sharpay. "Congratulations and thank you . . . Miss Sharpay Evans."

As surprised applause rippled through the theater, Sharpay winked at Ryan. She stepped forward to take her bow and turned to wave to Tiara, who was standing backstage with a dismayed expression on her face. Finally, Sharpay waved to her mom, then stepped back into the line.

Ms. Darbus waited until the audience had quieted down, then said, "And now, a senior who, I believe, has a decision to make. Mr. Troy Bolton. Troy?"

The spotlight hit Troy. "And I've chosen basketball," he announced.

Behind him, his friends all nodded. They had been expecting this.

"But I've also chosen theater," he revealed.

Eyebrows were raised as everyone wondered what this meant.

"The University of California in Berkeley offers me both," he said. "And that's where I'll be going next fall."

Now everyone was whispering to each other about this sudden twist. Everyone except Chad, that is, who looked totally shocked.

Troy reached for Gabriella's hand and gazed into her eyes. "Most of all, I choose the person who inspires my heart, which is why I picked a school that's exactly 32.7 miles from . . . you." He pulled her toward him so they could stand in the spotlight together. "Gabriella Montez," he said, making the announcement for Ms. Darbus. "Stanford University. School of Law."

For one long moment, Troy and Gabriella shared a look that seemed as if it might last forever.

Then the audience burst into applause, and Troy stepped back, allowing Gabriella to stand alone at center stage.

"Next, Mr. Chad Danforth, University of Albuquerque," Ms. Darbus said. "Basketball scholarship."

But as the audience cheered for Chad, his friends looked around, only to discover that the spot where he had been standing was now vacant.

"He's gone!" Taylor cried.

Troy didn't have to think twice. He knew exactly where Chad would be.

He took off running.

Sure enough, as Troy burst through the gym doors, he saw Chad on the court, wearing his cap and gown and shooting hoops.

Troy came to a stop and watched. How many hours had he and Chad spent in this gym, practicing, competing, laughing? As excited as Troy was about everything that lay ahead of him, he also felt a twinge of sadness at everything that would now be part of his past.

Chad seemed to be having the same thoughts.

He glanced at Troy and said, "So I guess when they hand us the diploma, we're actually done here."

"What makes you think we're getting diplomas?" Troy asked, trying to make a joke.

Chad gave him a faint grin in response. "One question. Does Berkeley play . . ."

"Yep, we're scheduled to kick the Redhawks' butts next November," Troy responded.

Chad's grin widened. So this wouldn't be the last time he and Troy were on the court together after all!

"Game on, hoops," he said.

They knocked fists—and then Troy stole the ball from Chad and went racing down the court, with his best friend right behind him. Before they knew it, they were laughing and doing their best to beat each other in a game of one-on-one. They had stopped thinking about what the future held, or how their friendship would change, or even what it would feel like to actually graduate.

Just then, a voice boomed through the gym. "Danforth! Bolton!" Coach Bolton yelled. "Get out there and get onstage!"

Troy stopped in his tracks and looked at Chad. "Now there's something I never thought I'd hear my dad say." He grinned.

They ran toward the gym door. As they passed Coach Bolton, he stopped Troy and gave him a proud look. Troy and his dad gave each other a quick hug. Now it was time to get to the stadium and graduate!

The football stadium was filled with parents, sisters, brothers, and friends as the Wildcats prepared for one last big moment at East High: graduation.

The seniors were lined up for their entrance, the buzz of happy laughter and conversation in the stadium was being shushed, and the processional was finally about to begin. This was it.

One by one, the Wildcats marched across the stage to get their diplomas, smiling broadly as their family and friends applauded for them. Suddenly, Troy stepped up to the podium to make an official address.

"East High is a place where teachers encouraged us to break the status quo and define ourselves as we choose." He glanced over at Ms. Darbus. "Where a jock can cook up a mean crème brûlée, and a brainiac can break it down on the dance floor. It's a place where one person, if it's the right person"—he looked over at Gabriella—"changes us all."

Troy cleared his throat and looked around at all his friends, the people he had gone to school with and had fun with and learned from. The people he would never forget.

"East High is having friends we'll keep for the rest of our lives. And that means we really *are*"— he grinned at the senior class—"all in this together. Once a Wildcat, *always* a Wildcat!"

Cheering, everyone threw their caps into the air and ran across the football field in celebration. The high spirits were contagious, and soon the senior class was singing and dancing, almost as if they couldn't leave East High without one last song. But as they reached the end of the field, the Wildcats turned around for one more look at the place that had changed their lives. After all, this was the end of high school—the end of four years of friendship and fun and of discoveries and changes that they couldn't have imagined on that first day at East High, which seemed like it was so long ago. They couldn't help wishing that, in some way, high school wouldn't end.

And then the Wildcats exited their stage for the very last time, on the way to meet their futures.

# EPILOGUE

Jimmie, Donny, and some other new members of the Wildcats bounded into the Wildcats locker room. It was the off-season, of course, and there wasn't a basketball practice scheduled, but they couldn't wait to get on the court and shoot some hoops.

They each opened up their lockers and found a basketball inside, with a combination written on it.

They turned at the same time to look at the lockers that Troy Bolton and Chad Danforth had used all during their high school careers as Wildcats.

Now Jimmie's and Donny's names were on the lockers, written on tape and stuck over Troy's and Chad's.

The two sophomores opened their new lockers and, with a little shiver of awe, discovered that each one held a pair of the rattiest, smelliest gym socks on the planet.

"They left us their lucky socks!" Jimmie exclaimed.

"Still haven't been washed," Donny whispered.

"Wow!" Jimmie was grinning from ear to ear. "Those dudes are so cool."

He and Donny looked at each other. Without asking, they knew they each had the same thought.

"What team?" Donny yelled.

"Wildcats!!!" Jimmie responded.

"What team?" Donny said again.

"Wildcats!" Jimmie responded.

"What team?" Donny shouted one last time.

"Wildcats!" Jimmie and the other players yelled. "Getcha head in the game!"

Everyone gave each other high fives. They couldn't wait for the new school year to begin.

PRESENTING

Disney

HIGH SCHOOL
MUSICAL
THE MUSICAL    THE SERIES

EAST HIGH

ROCK

STAR

Adapted by Sarah Nathan

Based on the episode "The Auditions"
by Tim Federle

# CHAPTER 1

Miss Jenn pulled her car into the faculty parking lot of East High. It was the first day of school, and she was excited to start her new job as the drama teacher. She breathed deeply and looked down at her phone.

"Oh, come on!" she said, hitting the screen. The buffering interrupted the song "We're All in This Together" from her favorite High School Musical movie. She looked up from the screen to the East High banner hanging over the school's front doors. She had seen those red-and-white letters so many times. And now here she was, ready to tackle the first day of school at the famous East High.

She got out of her car just as two boys on skateboards whizzed by her. She was pressed against the car.

"Sorry!" one called out.

"Our bad!" the other said.

"All good!" Miss Jenn said with a smile. "No bad!"

As she turned to head into the school, she didn't realize her dress was caught in the car door.

*Riiiiip.*

"Great, first costume change," Miss Jenn muttered to herself. She shook off the mishap and joined the stream of students heading inside the school.

Walking ahead of Miss Jenn were Ricky Bowen and his best friend, Big Red.

"Today's the day, Big Red," Ricky said. He was holding his skateboard and helmet in his hands. "It's happening."

"Junior year, baby," Big Red said, grinning. "Might grow a mustache. Might do a lotta things."

"Dude," Ricky said, turning to look at his red-headed friend. "I'm talking about Nini. Today's the day we start over."

Inside the school, Nini Salazar-Roberts walked down the hallway with her best friend, Kourtney, sharing stories about her summer at drama camp. "Oh, wait, I want to show you a picture," Nini said, holding her phone up. "This was my costume in act two."

"Flawless," Kourtney said. "Love it."

"And this is the wig that almost fell off in the middle of my ballad," Nini continued.

Down the hall, Ricky and Big Red made their way into East High. "We texted. She sounded neutral," Ricky told Big Red as they walked down the hall. "Nothing about bad news or needing to have a big talk. Just, 'Hey.' That's good, right?"

"Summers are no-man's-land, Ricky," said Big Red. "I don't know what 'Hey' means, and neither do you."

"I think it's good," Ricky said, trying to convince himself.

Nini and Kourtney continued their talk in front of Nini's locker. "And this . . ." Nini said.

Kourtney took the phone from Nini's hand. She zoomed in on the hot guy in the photo. "Oh, I know who that is, Nini," she said, smiling.

"Girl, I'm like point two seconds away from making that my lock screen," Nini said, with a twinkle in her eye. She turned to open her locker.

"I can't tell if you're glowing or you're sunburnt," Kourtney said.

Nini grinned. "Definitely glowing," she said. "I had the best summer ever."

"And what does . . . you-know-who have to say about all this?" Kourtney asked, leaning into her locker.

Nini took her phone back. "I'm waiting for the right time to tell him," she said.

"Yo! Nini!" Ricky said as he and Big Red approached the girls. "What's good?"

"How do you feel about right now?" Kourtney asked Nini.

"Hey," Ricky said.

"Hey," Nini replied. She took a deep breath. "Can we talk?" She didn't wait for his response. "I met someone at camp," she said. "I didn't plan—"

Ricky slumped. It had been his idea to take a

summer pause, but he hadn't thought that Nini would actually meet someone at drama camp. Sure, he had hung out with a couple girls over the summer, but all he had done was talk about Nini the whole time.

"Wait, is this a joke?" he said, interrupting her.

"Still talking here," Nini said with great confidence.

"Oh, snap!" Kourtney exclaimed with pride.

"I didn't plan for it to happen. But it happened," Nini told him. "He was the music man. I was Marian the librarian. It's called a show-mance."

Big Red was trying to keep up with the conversation. "Wait, you went to librarian camp? That's a thing?"

"Please tell me you're joking," Ricky said, staring at Nini.

"I'm not," Nini told him. She turned to face him and looked him straight in the eye. "Come on, Ricky. You know what you did. Or what you didn't do."

Unfortunately, Ricky knew exactly what she was talking about. There was no way either of them could forget that night in Nini's room when

391

she played the song for him. And how he had choked.

Under the twinkling lights strung across her room, the two had sat on Nini's bed watching skateboarding videos on Ricky's phone. Nini and Ricky had been dating for almost a year and she was happy—really happy. Sophomore year at East High had been pretty great with Ricky by her side.

Ricky looked up at her. "Do my feet stink?" he asked. He lifted his foot off the bed. "I feel like my feet stink."

"No," Nini said. Then she smiled. "Sort of," she said, shrugging and leaning in for a quick kiss. "I think it's cute."

Ricky laughed. "And that is why we work!"

Nini's heart melted. "Check your Instagram," she said, excited to share an anniversary message she had posted for him.

Ricky sat up and looked at his feed. Nini's post appeared. It was a video of her playing the ukulele and singing a song she wrote for him, mixed in with a montage of photos of the two of them over the past year. She wanted to tell Ricky that she loved him, and the song was the perfect way.

"I think I kinda, you know . . ." she sang sweetly. Then, at the end of the song, Nini leaned closer to him.

"I do, Ricky," she said. "I love you."

Ricky stared at her. His brown eyes were wide. And he was silent.

Now he was about to suffer the repercussions of that night.

"I . . . I don't believe this," Ricky said. He shook his head. "You're blowing me off for some theater punk you met four weeks ago? At a lake?"

"You kinda dumped me," Nini replied.

"It was a break! It wasn't a breakup," Ricky said.

"I'm sorry, Ricky, but it's a breakup now," she said.

"Hop off, girl," said Kourtney, clearly proud of her best friend.

"Stay out of it, Kourtney," said Big Red.

"You stay out of it," Kourtney replied. "I'm dismantling the patriarchy this year and I'm not afraid to start with you."

Nini turned and walked away with Kourtney by her side.

"You crushed it," Kourtney whispered to her. "That could not have gone better."

Nini smiled to herself. She felt good. She was Nini 2.0 and junior year was off to a good start, a really good start.

## WANT TO FIND OUT WHAT HAPPENS NEXT? WATCH

### Now streaming on

# Relive the Magic of
# HIGH SCHOOL MUSICAL

Popular star basketball player Troy Bolton and academically gifted beauty Gabriella Montez come from different worlds at East High. But when they both decide to audition for the school musical, magic happens! Follow Troy, Gabriella, and their friends as they navigate high school together in the Encore Edition of the junior novelizations from this beloved trilogy.

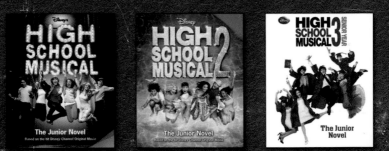

Then get a sneak peek of
*High School Musical The Musical: The Series*,
with bonus content from the all-new series
debuting on Disney+ in late 2019.

Disney ✦ PIXAR ✦ MARVEL ✦ STAR WARS ✦ NATIONAL GEOGRAPHIC

DISNEY PRESS

For more Disney Press fun, visit www.disneybooks.com

$7.99 US/ $10.49 CA

ISBN 978-136805910-7